CW01431230

Hannadelaneyauthor.com

To my husband and my girls,
for whom my love knows no bounds.

Oceanus

by Hanna Delaney

PROSPERO   You do look, my son, in a moved sort,
As if you were dismayed. Be cheerful, sir.
Our revels now are ended. These our actors,
As I foretold you, were all spirits and
Are melted into air, into thin air;
And – like the baseless fabric of this vision –
The cloud-capped towers, the gorgeous palaces,
The solemn temples, the great globe itself,
Yea, all which it inherit, shall dissolve,
And like this insubstantial pageant faded,
Leave not a rack behind. We are such stuff
As dreams are made on, and our little life
Is rounded with a sleep.

The Tempest, Act 4, Scene 1

1

November 2311

Born on Mars in the year 2290, Balthazar Swaine had the good fortune of growing up on a world greatly accustomed to space travel. His father, a mechanic for the Arden Space Corporation, was given accommodation and work on the bleak, sparsely populated planet in 2289. Having received no better offers on Earth, he took the job and raised his family offworld. Hamza Swaine was one of the first of many working class men to do so and through his career, had made many friends in high places on the back of his hard work and hard earned respect. Unlike his father before him, Balthazar had never been a particularly bright boy but he had made his father somewhat proud by joining the Starline cruiser, Demeter, as a cabin steward. Balthazar was short, infuriatingly slow-witted and unassuming but he showed promise. That was at least, according to the character reference written by a good friend of his father, Admiral James Winter. As the young man lacked many of the skills or personal characteristics required for almost any other occupation in the new worlds, Balthazar's parents were relieved to see him in paid employment. As for working hard, everyone who knew him felt that the young Mr Swaine had much farther to go.

It was probably considered gravely unlucky then that it should be Balthazar, the most overlooked man in all the galaxy, who was left to man the S.S Demeter alone on the morning of November 1st, 2311.

Fumbling through a manual for the communications systems on the bridge, he broke out into a sweat, flicking back and forth through pages and pages of a language he could barely read. The manual was written in the seven main languages of Earth: English, Spanish, Japanese, Mandarin, Hindi, Arabic and Bengali, however, it wasn't the language in particular that was troubling Balthazar. It was the fact that he felt he was being watched.

Finally, in an 'ah-ha' moment, Balthazar found the section that he was looking for. He then searched the panel in front of him and flipped a switch that said "LOG" above it. A red light flashed and the screen in front of him started recording through a front-facing camera. He started to speak into the microphone with heavy breath.

"This is Cabin Attendant Swaine of the Star Ship Demeter and it is 20:22 Earth time. I know that the ship's log isn't really my duty but there's no one else here." Swain took a swig of a bottle he had found earlier and pressed the record button again.

"Where do I start?

We were on a diplomatic voyage to visit the colonies of the Rimar and New Botswana and we have not arrived. I don't think we will ever get there." He looked anxiously over his shoulder as though he had heard something. Seeing that the bridge was empty, he continued.

"How do I explain this without it sounding highly suspicious? I can't! This makes no sense but fuck it, I might not live to hear it again." He took another gulp from the glass bottle. Balthazar knew that anyone watching would see 'that fat little idiot from housekeeping' and wouldn't believe him anyway; he had to try.

"The ship is deserted. I am sorry to say that I must have been asleep during what I can only describe as a strange occurrence. On finding that there was absolutely nobody on board according to the computer system, I personally searched some decks. There was no one in the captain's meeting rooms or his quarters. The XO is gone, as well." The workstations behind him were empty. The only things moving were the various scanners and lights, digits on the screens and the ship as it floated helplessly in orbit of the unknown planet below. He focused on the flickering red light of the recording.

"How I slept through all of this, I don't know and I don't remember it so stick with me." He rubbed his temples and leaned closer to the camera.

He lowered his voice to a whisper. "Cups of tea and coffee are half drunk, there are playing cards laid out still on the tables in the rec rooms. It's like the crew have vanished into thin air." He adjusted his tie and swallowed.

There was another pause. Swaine looked over his shoulder once more. The bridge remained—to his knowledge—empty. The windows revealed nothing but the vacuum of space outside. He shook his head and faced the camera again.

"Anyway, what I mean to say is that things are weird here and I can't really tell you what's happened. The Demeter is stuck here until further notice.

I don't know if this is some kind of sick joke or bad dream but I'm scared." He leaned back and gulped air this time. "There's something on this ship with me. I can't see it and haven't been able to trap it but I know it's there."

He held his breath for a moment. The only sound in the room was the heavy thumping of his heart which seemed to have crawled into the back of his throat, intent on choking him. Swaine's hands trembled and the hairs on the back of his neck stood up.

"You should also know that the diplomat in my charge was Owen Brennus, the governor of Atlantis and New Botswana's only hope of successful talks with the Rimar. I had one job and that was to keep Mr Brennus safe, fed, rested and occupied. It seems that I fell asleep on duty and I've lost him. For this, I am deeply sorry. I probably shouldn't have told you that but there's a chance that I'm going to die out here anyway. Dad, if you're watching this, I'm really sorry." He turned the recording off.

He stood as though to leave and quickly raised his finger, remembering something important. He dropped into the chair with a thump and turned the record button back on.

"I'm alone except for whatever this stowaway is. I'm scared. All right, I'm a bit tipsy too. Even the cat's gone. Christ, you don't think it ate the cat do you?" He began to cry in a drunken stupor.

"I've sent out a distress call and left it on loop. We were due to arrive at New Botswana by twenty-one hundred earth time on the 31st October, 2311. This gives me some hope that rescue crews on the Athena or the Artemis might come and look for us. Of course, this will only happen if war doesn't break out before that."

There was a clatter from somewhere inside the vents above him. Swaine didn't seem to notice it and kept talking.

"In the meantime, I need to try and find the access codes for the surveillance and scanners and see if they can tell me what has happened. To any crew who may be watching this, forgive me but I had to look everywhere for them. Trust me, I'd much rather be changing beds than searching through your cabins. End recording." he switched the recording off once more and stood up.

Exiting the bridge, he decided that he would lay out some traps to be safe. Something told him that his stowaway was bigger than a cat.

2

The sun shone with the illusion of a summer's day on a crisp November morning. Although it was a winter sun and lay too low in the icy-blue sky, it gave generously with what little morning light it had, bestowing it on the black loch below.

The white mist on the loch had risen to reveal a wooden dock, a small wooden row boat and a fisherman's sandstone cottage on the shore. Surrounding the cottage in a protective huddle were a mass of deciduous trees laced with hues of gold, red, green and brown.

Sitting on the edge of the dock with her long white feet submerged into the dark water was a young woman with hair as red as the leaves on the trees. She was enjoying the apricity of the sunshine and gently swirling the water with one foot as the ebony waves lapped against the posts. In another time, the girl could have been mistaken for a naiad.

Most days, she liked to have an early morning swim in the loch. There were some mornings where she preferred to just dip a toe in, or a foot or both feet. However it happened, a jolt of cold water and fresh air was what was needed to wake her up properly after a night of vivid dreams.

The silence was soothing. Only the quiet, cool rush of air or the faint singing of birds could be heard in the distance until there was an unexpected clap of thunder and a flash of lightning.

"Thea!" called a man's voice from the cottage. "Thea, come inside now."

The girl stood up and immediately ran to the cottage with the swift grace of a gazelle.

"What is it, father?"

"There's a storm coming and I don't want you to get caught up in it," he said, closing the door behind her. Her father was Derrien Victor Smith; he was a tall, gruff looking man. He had once told his daughter that his name was Greek for "prosperous" or "great." Sometimes, she felt that the man standing before her was everything but prosperous or great. He had deep lines across his brow and weatherbeaten skin from years of outside toil. His sun-bleached, threadbare shirt was missing buttons at the collar and heavily creased. The cloak that he wore any time he ventured outside looked tattered and moth-eaten and it smelled worse than a dead dog on a pavement in the height of summer. She studied him for a moment while he busied himself striking matches and lighting beeswax candles around the room, aided sporadically by flashes of lightning.

The sky outside blackened and with its enormous shadow, suspended itself over the loch and the cottage. The girl, her porcelain face fixed, watched from the window.

"What a strange storm," she observed.

The sudden downpour of rain pelted against the window. Thea tried to peer out into the blackened abyss.

When she could make out the outline of the darkened sky, bright, dazzling sparks flashed to reveal a series of what at first seemed like shooting stars. They left trails of white smoke behind them as they floated down into the atmosphere with the grace of dandelion seeds blown by the wind. The shapes scattered and seemed to land in various locations across the island.

The waves crashed furiously against the dock as the wind and rain competed to see who could wreak the most havoc. She stood there, still, huddled, watching the storm in controlled awe like a child at a formal gathering.

"Father, what are those things in the sky?" she asked, pointing to the shapes as they fell one by one.

"Thea, do you remember when we first came here? It was during a storm like this."

"I was a child, wasn't I? I barely remember."

"What you're seeing before you is something that's going to put it all right. Did you know that your father was once a great man? A world-leading scientist?"

His daughter looked him up and down, tilting her head in bemusement. "Are you not my father?" she asked.

"Oh I am, dear girl. I was always your father. Your mother was a goddess among women. We lived happily in a grand house with our own staff, you know."

"Why did we come here, then? Why do we now wear rags?" She glanced at her own tattered dress that she had made herself out of discarded canvas.

"Foul play. There were those who sought to destroy me and banish me from their sight." His features darkened as he fixed his stare on the window.

"And I, too?" Thea asked, tearing him from his daydream.

"They tried to take you from me. Your mother had perished and you would only sleep if I was with you, so I brought you everywhere with me. The shuttle that we were on was sabotaged. You were always meant to be with me."

"Do you know who sought to destroy you, father?" She looked at the old man in wonder.

"Aye. My wretched brother and his minions."

Another bolt of lightning hit the loch. Thea looked out once more.

She had not known what she had seen until one of the stars was headed in her direction. It was then that she realised they had not been stars but they were in fact shuttles. One particular shuttle was hurtling toward her and crashed into the loch.

"Father, what have you done?"

"Only what I needed to do. No one will be harmed. I promise."

"The men on *that* shuttle will." She pointed to the sinking grey object in the middle of the loch.

A pang of panic set in at this point as he felt his daughter's judgement. The old man paused for a moment. "Thea, go and save those men in the loch."

"Very well, father."

She left the house and ran back to the dock.

At first, the waves were too high for her to capture sight of the shuttle clearly. Only when they started to subside did she see that it had started to sink. The water glugged greedily, pulling the helpless vessel down into the black depths. A break in the clouds brought with it a small beam of light that revealed a grey bow still visible for a few more seconds until the loch consumed that too.

What felt like hours later, there was a splash and a gasp for air coming from the middle of the loch.

Thea, without hesitation, dived in and swam to the origin of the movement, cutting through the wind's currents as best she could in her heavy clothes. She found a body vigorously thrashing and flailing and dragged it to the surface with all of her strength, kicking her legs with everything she had.

She had rescued a young man, and in the darkness she could not tell if he was or wasn't breathing. She swam on her back, holding him so that his face was turned up toward the sky. When she reached the shore of the loch she heaved him onto his front. He spluttered water and gasped for more air, coughing and retching into the sand. His fingernails were filthy from clutching the earth as he scrambled to his hands and knees. His face was red and he was coughing profusely. She placed her hand on his shoulder and helped him to sit down.

He looked at her blankly, paused for a moment and turned away to vomit into a nearby shrub. He then fainted, landing with a thud onto the ground beneath him. The rain was lessening now and the light was returning to the loch.

As the young woman stood over the unconscious survivor, she studied his uniform. It was a fine royal blue jacket over royal blue trousers. His boots were black and although sodden, seemed new. On his left breast he wore a gold pin badge. It was a symbol that she did not recognise. The gold trim of his jacket and trousers suggested that he was someone of importance. She observed how unusual the boy looked compared with the other people she had known on the island. She had never seen anyone dressed like that.

Thea hadn't noticed that it had stopped thundering or that the sky was clear again. As though on cue, thick clouds parted, opening up like a stage curtain; the birds returned to their songs and the loch was as still as it had been before the crash.

"Thea!" Her father was approaching.

She looked back at the gentleman she had rescued. He was still unconscious. "Thea! Are they alive?" asked Derrien with growing concern. He was wearing the old, stinking cloak over his peasant clothing now. In contrast to the boy, her father's boots were torn and full of holes, talking as he walked. For the first time in her life, she felt embarrassed to look upon him.

"There was only one," she said, glancing back at the half-drowned boy and then at the sky. "The storm... it's gone."

"How peculiar," her father agreed. "Let's get him inside."

"Is this your brother?"

"No, my child. Far too young. Come, let's get this poor wretch inside."

3

"I could kill that steward," Anthony Victor Smith barked as he wrestled with vines and ferns.

"What steward?" asked Seb. Seb Mariner was the security assistant of the Atlantean governor. He was a tall, thin man with hawkish features and a crop of black hair sat atop his long, gaunt face.

"That crewman who told me to get into the shuttle. What a muppet."

"Was there? I don't recall a steward?"

"Yes, there was a housekeeping steward. Told me to get into the shuttle. Didn't know what was going on yet spoke to me like I was *his* inferior," he hissed.

"I don't recall, sir. The crash is still a blur for me."

"And me," added Ade, the ship's doctor.

"Yes, all right" Anthony waved his hand as though shooing flies. "I barely remember it either. I just recall that bloody twit for some reason. He must have been out of line. I should have him sent to a penal colony," he grumbled. "Anyway, where the hell are we?" Anthony was a hot-headed, olive-skinned man in his fifties. He was an imposing figure, broad-shouldered and never without a sneer. Staff remarked that he looked more like a mafia boss than a scientific adviser but looks could be deceiving. He seemed to have earned the trust of the governor in spite of all his apparent flaws.

Seb responded with a sigh. "No idea, sir."

"Comms signals?" asked Anthony, the irritation in his voice growing.

"None sir. There is either no reception or our signals are being blocked." Ade, as the ship's doctor, was carrying the emergency kit with flares, medication and a Personal Locator Beacon. The PLB was unresponsive. "It's not ideal."

"The Rimar?" Anthony turned to Trin Rowan this time. Trin was the scientific adviser's assistant and hoped that she would one day herself become a scientific adviser to a colony. She was a small, young woman with short, blonde curly hair and a well freckled, friendly, welcoming face.

"I don't know," she shook her head and aimed her scanner out at the surrounding flora again. "We have no idea who is behind this, sir. We're on a planet that appears to be perfectly habitable but doesn't appear on our records as a terraformed world. This jungle is... well look at it." They each observed the dense foliage and the established roots underfoot, hearing various sounds belonging to wildlife. "There is humidity in the air and quite obviously an ecosystem which is impressive but...there are no recognisable landmarks. We're lost," Trin remarked. "I keep thinking that I'm in some sort of dream. I wouldn't have imagined this would happen in a million years but here we are! What an opportunity!" Her enthusiasm was not catching on.

Anthony, sensing his own impatience bubbling as it approached boiling point, was in no mood for Trin's optimism. He waved his hand again in annoyance, "Tell me, Seb, do you have any ideas?" he asked, turning to look at Owen's assistant. Seb was gone. "Seb?" he demanded. His voice travelled nowhere in the dense jungle.

"Come back at once! You can't pull stunts like this out here," he called, his voice catching the impending fear. No one responded. As though a switch had flicked off, there was a sudden onset of silence. It deepened, sending tingles through Anthony's limbs. A chilling wind rubbed against his ears, followed by the stiffening of the hairs on the back of his neck. He surrendered to the rush of blood rising in his mouth, tightening in his throat. Anthony turned to look in the direction of some ferns that were rustling. "Seb?"

Out from behind the ferns, he was ambushed by an enormous beast. Anthony froze. *Run. Run!* he thought, but his trembling legs wouldn't move. Finally, as the creature lunged toward him, he rolled away, scrambled up and produced the first stick that he could clutch. Seeing only teeth and fur and feeling his life flash before his eyes, he thwacked the beast down while it was mid-lunge and he collapsed with a yowl onto the floor, limbs shaking. Knowing that his strike would have only aggravated his predator, he looked up to meet death. To his surprise, there was nothing there.

"Anthony? Where are you?" It was Owen Brennus, the governor. With him were Trin, Seb and Ade. On seeing Anthony on the ground and now in the foetal position, Owen asked, "What happened to you?"

"You all disappeared! Then there was this bloody tiger thing!" His heart raced to a point where he felt it would overdo it. He tried desperately to steady his breath.

"Tiger?" asked Owen, his brow raised.

"A bloody tiger! It was monstrous. A prehistoric one!"

They all looked around to see if there were any paw prints or claw marks nearby. "Sir, there's nothing here. Are you sure?" asked Trin.

"No, I'm just lying on the floor because I'm tired, Trin," he said sarcastically with a scowl.

Unconvinced but nonetheless concerned, Owen helped him to his feet. "It's a strange place, I know. I didn't see what you saw but I have seen things, too." He patted Anthony on the shoulder with a large, strong hand. Owen was himself an imposing figure. Standing at six feet and seven inches tall with a dark, brooding countenance, Owen could make his presence known in any situation.

"Like what?" Anthony asked.

"Well, you disappeared for a start!" Owen's eyes were smiling now.

"Did I? You disappeared from me more like." Anthony cringed at his own accusatory tone. He respected his governor and tried his utmost never to reveal his temper to him.

"There was this grassy wall that appeared all of a sudden and then when we heard you screaming, it went "poof" just like that," said Trin in an animated fashion. "We're definitely seeing things. I'll be the first to admit it."

"I have seen Geraint. He appears to me and vanishes again. He doesn't speak. He looks well." Owen's voice trailed off. "He looks well..."

Anthony watched Owen's eyes lower. "Governor Brennus," he began, "I'm sure he is safe and well."

Owen said nothing but nodded with a rueful grin. "Anyway," he said, snapping out of it. "We must press on if we are ever to find the way through." He pointed north and began walking. The party followed in silence.

"I don't believe this," Anthony remarked as he stamped his foot in an uncontrollable rage. They had arrived back where they were just hours before. The team of survivors, exhausted and hungry, looked around with mixed expressions of dismay and frustration.

"We can set up camp for tonight. That's all we can do," Owen said with a defeated shrug.

As the darkness started to set in and the other members of the team took it in turns to sleep, Anthony Victor Smith sat up, alert. An expert in his field, Anthony had been highly revered for anticipating every scenario possible in every possible context; his skills had left him forever suspicious of his surroundings, and on this particular night, Anthony sensed that they were not alone.

4

— · —

As well as a fisherman's cottage and a black loch, there was also a woodsman's hut near the centre of the island. As Derrien Victor Smith approached the hut, he saw that a young man with long, braided black hair was chopping logs in front of the hut. His shirtless, bare skin was tanned and red from hours in the sun. He was hunched over and sweating.

"Jet," called Derrien to the man. "I need some more firewood, please."

"It's there," the young man said nonchalantly, pointing to a pile of chopped firewood that was right next to where Derrien was standing. He did not look up from his work. Sensing that the young man was in no mood for conversation, Derrien hung there, twiddling his fingers.

"The weather is quite good this week, isn't it?"

The young man shrugged and continued with his work. Derrien, not wanting to give up just yet, tried again. "Jet, can't we talk?" he asked.

"I have nothing to say to you." Jet seemed heavily inconvenienced by the presence of his landlord.

"Please, Jet," pleaded the old man. "I've only ever wanted to be your friend."

Friend. The word infuriated Jet. He looked up and straightened, adopting an intimidating stance, his axe resting over his shoulder. Derrien felt himself shrink away.

"Friends?" He looked down at Derrien, disgusted.

"Friends, Jet. Every day I am sorry about what has come between us. We can't let it—"

"You can't even speak her name." The fury was building in the young man's body, reddening his face.

"She was evil, Jet," Derrien said quietly.

"She was my mother!" he roared, menacingly squaring up to his aggravator.

"Just read the journals, Jet." Derrien raised his hands and began to back away. "You'll see why I had to do it. Then you could talk to me—"

"Talk to *you*?" Jet was incandescent with fury. He threw his axe into the X on the ground with alarming accuracy. "I will never, ever talk to my mother's murderer." He turned to face Derrien, "you are scum. You are a plague on Oceanus- my island! It was hers and now it is mine. You come here and you take what isn't yours." Jet's voice grew impassioned and emotional as he pointed at Derrien, forcing him to walk backwards some more. "This was nothing to do with you. She took you in, let you learn our ways and now you prance around here like you own the place. I hate you. I *hate* you." Jet tried to lunge but just as he did, he caught himself and held his head, crying out in pain.

"Please, Jet, don't do this—" Derrien begged.

"What have you done to me?" Jet cried. He was crippled with agony.

"Jet," Derrien pleaded, "Just calm down, Jet"

"Get away from me! Take your firewood and leave." Jet spat at Derrien's feet and ran off into the woods.

Derrien returned to the cottage to find the other young man on the island still asleep on a makeshift bed under the window. He was tossing and turning in his sleep.

"Thea," whispered Derrien, looking over to the kitchen. Thea came floating into the room.

"He is alive, father. That crash must have really distressed him." She looked down at the sleeping guest.

"Do you know his name yet?"

"I don't. He hasn't really come to. He opens his eyes every now and then but he hasn't said anything and doesn't respond when I speak to him."

"He nearly drowned, I suppose," Derrien shrugged. He thought of the other survivors, scattered on the island. *What a mess*, he thought, looking at the boy. *I could have killed him.*

"I am glad," said Derrien sadly. "I must go and do some work now. I will be back in the morning. Do not answer the door to anyone."

"Of course, father."

***

Journal of D Victor Smith November 1, 2311

Subject REL and I seem to be merged. Some sort of symbiosis. Today at the hut, the boy tried to strike me and was paralysed by what could have been a headache? He wouldn't say. He was in great pain but couldn't hurt me. Somehow, REL can control the weather. I have no way of proving this as yet but I think REL can control Jet too. Perhaps it can block others— I don't know.

Whatever Lennox did with REL, it had the opposite effect of what happened with me. I wonder if it is genetic, psychic, or luck? Why scram-

ble her brain but share everything with mine? Must investigate further.
REL seems calm and accepting of my presence. The creature has suffered
greatly.

The other boy is a concern. Have yet to learn where he fits. He is in
Althea's charge for now but they will be looking for him. I must be ready.

5

— · —

Just behind the little cottage on the loch was a walled garden with charming sandstone brickwork. Ivy and climbing roses intertwined before they parted off in different directions. Birds of all colours and sizes visited regularly, taking advantage of the insects in abundance. In recent decades, despair was a common feeling among those concerned with nature but in the newly discovered worlds, flora and fauna could grow and thrive.

Thea cared for her garden every day. Although it was November, the flowers blossomed as though it were May in the northern hemisphere of Earth.

She was watering tulips that stood at the foot of a magnificent magnolia tree when her guest entered the garden. "Hello," he said.

Thea turned her head sharply to identify the voice. It was the young man, completely dry as well as looking healthier now that the colour had returned to his face. He was taller than he had seemed when lying down, and the gold on his uniform's trim was impressive in the mid-morning light. She stared at him. The young stranger was fascinating.

Her rosebud lips parted to reveal a gleaming set of teeth as she gave what he understood to be a genuine, friendly smile. "Are you feeling better?" she asked.

"I mean, my head hurts a bit but I'm feeling much better. Thank you for saving my life." He held out his hand. Thea, not knowing what this meant, tilted her head. She reluctantly mirrored him, holding out hers too. Geraint Brennus, on seeing that handshakes may not have been customary in this strange place, held her hand and initiated the handshake anyway. Her hand was soft and limp, and she looked down at it as though it was in possession of its own behaviours. His hand felt cool and strong in hers.

"I am Geraint," he said softly. "How do you greet people here?" He let go of her gently.

"We just say hello. I only embrace my father, really." The girl shrugged and looked at him intently.

"Your father?"

"Yes, my father helped me to rescue you. He's gone now but he'll be back later."

"I look forward to thanking him too. Please forgive me but I don't know your name?"

"It's Thea. Well, it's actually Althea, but everyone calls me Thea." Her head tilted again with a smile.

"Althea." He thought that she had a beautiful name. "And this is your garden?" He looked around in awe. It was spectacularly alive with birds, butterflies and dragonflies.

She nodded proudly. It was a sight to behold, even for someone who was used to professionally maintained grounds and gardens. "I never realised one person could keep such a lovely garden," he remarked, gently holding the yellow daffodil heads in his hands and releasing them. A bee buzzed past his eyes in slow motion, its black furry legs saddled with fresh pollen. Everything in the garden was a feast for his eyes, including the gardener. She was tall, auburn haired and had the loveliest face that he had ever seen.

"We're lucky here. There is plenty of food without having to farm the land."

"What kind of things do you eat?"

"There are orchards, plenty of fish and animals to hunt. Father also prints a lot of food for us."

"He has a food printer?" Geraint was interested now. Perhaps this place wasn't as technologically far from home as it seemed.

"It's all the same seaweed but at least it tastes of something else each time," she said with a giggle. Her laugh tinkled like a bell. Geraint was entranced. "Tell me, where did you come from?"

"Oh," he put his hands in his pockets. "Atlantis," he said. "Do you know it?" She shook her head.

"Really? You've never heard of it?"

"I don't think so. What's it like?"

"It's a water planet I guess. It has cities and islands but it's mostly water... and hot. It's almost always hot."

"We have a lot of water here, too!" she said excitedly.

"I know, I drank a fair amount of it." He smiled. After a slight delay, she laughed enthusiastically, almost forcefully. Geraint looked uncertain but smiled at her regardless, lifting a corner of his mouth. He thought that she was beautiful albeit quite strange.

They sat down on a bench overlooking the flowerbeds of tulips, alliums and roses. Sitting closer to his rescuer, Geraint could study her face in greater detail. Her skin could have been made of the most delicate porcelain. Her thick wavy hair looked soft and made from the finest silk in all the universe, catching glimmers of light like embers.

Geraint confidently turned his body towards her. Her large round eyes were pools of wonder and she was looking right at him. She smiled again.

There was a brief pause. The pair were now sitting even closer to each other, gazing into one another's eyes. His were dark, brooding and full of hunger. Hers, full of curiosity. Geraint leant in and pursed his lips, placing his hand on her waist. Surprised at his sudden behaviour, she leaned back from him.

"Why did you do that?" she asked, matter of factly.

Geraint removed his hand. "I am sorry, I thought you wanted me to."

"Why did you do that?" she asked again, plainly.

Geraint's face flushed crimson. "I said I was sorry.

"But I don't understand, why did you touch me?"

Much to his chagrin, he answered her, "I thought you wanted me to."

"I didn't say anything." The girl seemed baffled.

The boy didn't know what to say or what to do. As the young, charismatic son of a governor, he had never met a girl who did not want him to kiss her. This particular girl was strange to him, growing stranger by the minute. She was staring with what now felt more like overly large, too-blue eyes. Her angelic face suddenly seemed excessively doll-like and he started to feel uncomfortable. At that moment, she seemed incredibly alien to him. Rejection was alien to him.

"I must go now. My father will be looking for me," he said sheepishly, shuffling away.

"You have a father too?" she asked. This seemed to delight her.

"Yes. My father is Owen Brennus. He's the governor of Atlantis. We crash landed here. Well, I think he did too. Have you seen him?"

"No. Even if I had, I'm not really supposed to talk to strangers."

Geraint's eyes narrowed slightly and he rubbed his forehead. "Thea, how old are you?"

"Seventeen. How old are you?"

"Seventeen." He looked at her searchingly. She did look like a girl who would be a similar age to him but something about her manner threw him off. *This planet and its people are strange,* he thought.

"How long have you been here?" he asked.

"Since I can remember. My father and I were abandoned here when I was a little girl. A nice scientist and her son took us in. She's gone now but Jet is still here."

"Jet, is he–?"

"Is he what?"

"Is that why you didn't want me to touch you, because of Jet?"

"I don't understand." She tilted her head again, frowning slightly.

"Is Jet your friend?"

"Yes. I think so." She nodded even if she still seemed puzzled.

Geraint felt that he wasn't going to get the answers he needed, so he changed the subject. "Thea, please can you help me find my father?"

"I'm not sure if I can."

"Why not?"

"Father hasn't told me to."

"You need to ask your father?"

"Yes. I always ask my father."

"Do you do everything he tells you to?"

"Of course. I *am* obedient."

6

— • —

By early morning, the mist from the loch was in full opacity, suspended over the black water like a white phantom. The sun rose slowly, casting its bright dawn sunshine on the front window of the sandstone cottage. Derrien had returned, passing the front window like a shadow as he approached the cottage door. He had seen that Thea was sitting with their guest at the fireside. The pair had been talking quietly, their bodies leaned in toward each other.

Derrien gently closed the door with a click. Thea stood to attention.

"Father," she said happily. She hurried to embrace him in the doorway of the sitting room, kissing him on the cheek. His face was cold and reddening in the heat of the cottage's sitting room.

"I'm very sorry, my dear. I had some errands to run." He embraced the girl tightly and buried his face into her bouncing waves of auburn hair.

"Father, you're squeezing me," Thea whispered.

"Oh, I'm so sorry." He backed away and turned to observe the guest sitting down in the corner by the fire. The young man had been staring, studying father and daughter with his dark, penetrating eyes.

Geraint's first impressions of the man were that he thought he looked haggard, bone-tired and bewildered all at once. He also found himself instinctively wanting to know where Derrien had managed to go and busy himself in such a secluded place. He had only known of Thea, her father and the elusive Jet. There seemed to be no one else.

Realising that he was being rude, Geraint stood up quickly and extended a hand. "I'm Geraint. Thea has told me so much about you, Mr Victor Smith."

"Welcome, Geraint." Derrien crossed the small room to shake the young man's hand enthusiastically. "It's good to see that you're up and about. Have you been well provided for?" Geraint could see that Derrien, despite his dishevelled look, had been a handsome man once. The lines across his forehead and eyes ran deep and provided a stark pale contrast to his established tan. His teeth were the tidiest thing about him.

"Absolutely. Thea has been so kind." Geraint looked at the girl for a moment as though it was the first time. She had been kind. She had been trusting. She had welcomed him and cared for him. He felt that this was the first time in his life that anyone had done anything for him and asked for nothing in return. Thea continued to baffle him but he couldn't help but feel a growing sense of fondness for her company. Geraint found that her sunny disposition was hard to shun, no matter how depressing his predicament was.

"Excellent." Derrien softly smiled at his daughter who was gazing at the young Geraint. Whether Geraint was aware of the girl's feelings or not, he didn't let on in front of her father. Geraint watched Derrien remove his cloak and Thea took it away to hang somewhere. Geraint, mildly relieved that the smell was now leaving the room, admired Thea's ability to act completely unfazed by things that were normally considered offensive to the senses. Geraint reflected that Thea herself smelled of fresh air and flowers from her garden.

"Tell me, Geraint," Derrien said, sitting down in the armchair by the fire. "How did you come to be here?" He crossed his legs and fixed his attention on the young man, who stood twiddling his fingers as though preparing for an interrogation. Geraint eventually took the armchair opposite and warmed his hands by the flames.

"By accident," he shrugged. "I didn't know that there was even a planet out here."

"Well, we have that in common," Derrien said with a hollow laugh.

"We were headed for New Botswana. I don't remember everything. I must have hit my head or something but I believe that there was a breach in the hull of our ship, the Demeter. Alarms were going off, people were shouting and running here, there and everywhere. I was in my cabin reading when the alarm started and within seconds there was a knock on my door. It was a room attendant shouting for me.

He said that I had to hurry and get into a shuttle. I asked where my father was but the guy didn't know. He just insisted I had to leave before the ship fell apart. It was terrifying, really. By the time I got to the shuttle bay there were hardly any left. There was smoke everywhere.

I didn't even have to pilot the thing. It was set to autopilot. The turbulence was making me feel sick." Geraint stopped himself and placed his hand on the crown of his head. He felt a tender lump there under his wavy, dark brown hair. "I did hit my head," he said quietly. He remembered that it had been bleeding. "I don't remember anything after that. I woke up here and Thea... Thea was there." He looked over his shoulder for Thea. She was in the back kitchen shuffling about and clattering some crockery.

After some time, Derrien asked, "do you know where you are?"

"Oceanus. Thea told me. That's the name of the island, right?"

"The entire planet. The planet is called Oceanus," Derrien assert-ed. "The first settlers here believed it was where dreams came from. There's nothing here but the ocean and this lonely little island."

"When did you come here?"

"Fifteen years ago." Derrien stood up solemnly. He walked to the window and peered out at the early morning sun coming up over the trees. "Just Thea and I." His back was turned away from his young inquisitor.

"It was raining that night. Very similar to how it was when you came here, actually. She was so small." His eyes were tearing up and he forced himself to swallow a lump that was rising in his throat. "It was awful." Derrien stopped for a moment and shook his head. He looked out onto the loch and remembered the very night that he and his tiny child had been dropped from the sky themselves in an emergency shuttlecraft with nothing but the clothes on their backs and a box of Derrien's belongings. His sadness turned to rage, transforming his hands into fists at his sides.

They were lucky enough to have made a safe landing but the storm, he felt, had been relentless. He cradled his frightened, crying child all that night until the following morning when the storm had subsided.

That was when Shona Lennox had found them.

She had called to the shuttle first, gently, so that those inside knew not to be afraid. She carried with her a stack of blankets and a basket of food. Derrien thought back to her angular, handsome face as she greeted him and his little girl for the first time.

No more, he thought. He could not think about Shona Lennox right now.

"Sorry... Where was the ship on its way to again?" Derrien turned to look at Geraint. He had forgotten most of the conversation as well as he had forgotten most things recently. The boy looked confused, watching him from across the room.

"W-we were on our way to New Botswana. My father was hosting talks there."

"Your father? Who is he? I wonder if I know him."

"He's Owen Brennus, Lord Governor of Atlantis," the boy said.

The adrenaline rushed through Derrien's body on hearing the name *Brennus*. His cheeks were flushed and his mouth felt dry, reducing him to nothing more than a pulse. The blood thrashed around his head as he tried to think. He had not realised Brennus had a son. The offspring of his enemy sat in his living room, about to drink tea with an added lump of sweet oblivion.

For a few minutes, Derrien did not speak. The silence nestled itself between them. Geraint was shuffling in his chair, looking back to the kitchen in the hope that Thea would reappear. "Atlantis was my home," Derrien finally said, quietly.

Geraint's expression brightened immediately. "It was? You must know him then."

"Not really," Derrien lied, looking away.

"I see," Geraint, having talked about his father, was swamped with feelings of sadness and despair. He looked away at the fire for a moment. Derrien observed that the son of Owen Brennus was also a tall, dark haired character with a brooding look about him. He wondered if deceitfulness was a family trait, but the boy for the time being seemed innocent enough.

"I haven't seen my father since we were on the Demeter," Geraint said.

"I don't suppose you have." Derrien thought for a moment. "You're the only one I've been able to find," he admitted apologetically.

A darkness crossed Geraint's face as he looked at Derrien. "There is still time," he declared. "I would be very grateful if you could help me find him."

Thea had returned to the sitting room with a tray of tea and laid it on the table. She poured a cup for her father and brought it to him. Derrien covered his forehead with one hand and waved her off with the other. "I'm sorry my dear, no tea for me. I have a headache. Probably should get some shut-eye."

She seemed crushed. "Of course, father."

"I'll have some tea with you," Geraint smiled. Thea turned to him and handed him the cup. What he felt for Thea overall, he wasn't entirely sure but he found that he hated the thought of her having her feelings hurt. His offer of tea seemed to brighten her face again.

"Forgive me. I will catch up with you later." Derrien backed out of the room and slid upstairs.

"What would you like to do today then?" Geraint asked, trying not to think of his father or the strange interaction that had passed between himself and Derrien.

"What is there to do around here, anyway?"

"Oh." Thea thought for a moment, her chin resting on her thumb and forefinger. Geraint thought that her mannerisms were adorable, even if they were exaggerated and sometimes strange to him. "Perhaps I could show you the island?" she offered.

"I'd really love that."

"We could go to the beach. I used to collect shells there when I was a little girl. Perhaps we could see what's there today."

Chapter 7

It had been twenty-four hours since Anthony had last slept, or so he thought. The sun had disappeared some time before. The birds and their varied calls had changed, becoming more ominous, more unsettling. The scurrying shadows of small rodents shot across the floor of the jungle and darted up various trees with a swish. The crackling fire had provided much needed warmth for the travellers as they dozed. The glowing heat had warmed Anthony's back through the night as he sat, holding his knees and looking out into the darkness, but no longer.

This was not the first time he had had strange dreams; this was not the first time that he had been in a jungle, and this was not his first time in a hostile place. It was, however, the first time he had been left alone with his demons.

The other survivors in the incongruous jungle had taken it in turns to sleep and take on the watch. Anthony stayed on watch the entire time, whether it was his turn or not. His eyes were bloodshot and sunken. His hair, standing on end after countless finger strokes. His heavy jaw remained shut. He did not know how long he had been there but suddenly he noticed that the chill of early morning was upon him and permeated through the camp, causing those sleeping to stir and those already stirred to shiver.

Why am I here? What has brought me to this hellhole?

Deep in his heart, he knew why. He knew that his career and his success had come at a cost. A human cost. He felt that he deserved it; he did not want to think about that right now. The jungle was an alien place. He must be on guard. He fought back the intrusive thoughts. *Thoughts can't kill you.*

The fire that Trin had made was dying, stifled in the dampness of the pre-dawn gloom. He started to shiver uncontrollably.

Stay awake. The sun is coming. We can regroup and get out of this place. Stay awake. Stay the hell awake, man. For God's sake, no. Don't fall asleep.

A dull pang punched him hard in the gut. He looked up and could not see anything but black, as though he had been transported away to a damp, dark cave and hadn't noticed. The end of his nose was chilled to numbness. He could still hear the shuffling of his sleeping companions and the occasional scurrying of the jungle's nocturnal creatures but he could see nothing but his icy, white breath escaping from his mouth and the darkening light before him.

Anthony's eyes were pinned to a shadow sitting directly across from him. The shadow, he realised, did not belong to him. It couldn't have belonged to him because this shadow had eyes.

Dread sat heavy now. In his new state of terror, Anthony tried to move a finger. Nothing. He was paralysed.

Even when Trin and Seb had started moving around, dressing and rolling up their sleeping bags, Anthony could not call to them. His mouth was fixed shut.

You're asleep. Wake up. Come on, wake up!

Anthony tried in vain to fight against the fatigue, eyes remaining open: eyes remaining fixed on the shadowed figure in front of him.

"Murderer," it whispered. Its hiss seeped into his skin, tingling under the surface like the venom of a snake.

Anthony tried to move away but his legs remained set in stone. Helpless. His head, rendered immobile. A demonic hand gripped his head and forced him to face the shadow.

"Murderer" It was talking to him now in a man's voice. A voice he felt he recognised but could not think to place. "Murderer." Its hoarse accusations grew louder. "Murderer!" The shadow grew larger with every second that Anthony didn't fill with a response. It opened up its wings and hovered over him, swamping him in cold, heavy darkness. Anthony gasped for air as the apparition smothered him with its freezing, black emptiness. His lungs wouldn't open.

You're not real. You're not real.

"Murderer," it repeated, enveloping him in a chilling abyss. Anthony still could not move away, fight himself free or look anywhere else. He closed his eyes as a final act of protest.

"You're not real. Go away. Go away. Go away!" he wanted to cry. The beads of sweat rolled down his nose and cheeks. He was unable to scratch or wipe the sweat away, making it itch all the more.

The shadow grew even larger than before, consuming him. Anthony tried with all his strength to wave it away; his arms would not do as he wanted.

You're not fucking real. Fuck off.

"I am real."

Its hands clenched his neck within an iron grip. He thought of his mother and another face that was not hers but the face of someone else he had once loved. He was a little boy again, playing football with another little boy in a green back garden with goal posts and a garden hose. A brother. He stifled a sob. His muscles were going into a convulsion.

Please, no.

"Sir?" It was Trin, shaking him gently. Anthony opened his eyes with alarm. Trin and Seb were standing over him as he lay on the floor, their brows furrowed with concern. "Are you alright? You were shouting in your sleep. We thought you were having a seizure so we had to wake you." Trin could not ignore the look of terror in Anthony's eyes. He was pale, shivering and barely able to get a fix on his surroundings.

"I wasn't asleep! Anthony looked straight at Trin, his eyes bloodshot. "I've been awake all night." Weakly, he stood up and dusted himself off.

"Sir..." Trin's voice was soft and sympathetic. "You've been asleep since we made camp. We didn't want to wake you after the incident," she said quietly. "Ade suggested you should rest as much as possible." Her amiable, freckled face made Anthony feel even more ridiculous than before. She placed a hand on his arm. He was trembling.

"Oh." Anthony felt his face flush crimson. "This place is like a nightmare," he reflected as he sat back down again. "We have to get out of here." Seb and Trin each gave a receptive nod. Seb rounded up the others and the party packed up their camping equipment.

"Sir, we're going to get out of here." Trin had come to help him gather his kit and pack up. Her kindness hurt him deeply; he felt that he was not worthy of it.

"Don't worry Trin, I can take care of this."

"Sir..." She spoke firmly this time. "Let me help you." It was a demand more than a polite insistence; he did not have the strength to argue with her and held up his hands in surrender. "You know, I used to have this sleep paralysis thing," she said in a low voice, rolling his mat up. "People thought I was crazy. I just couldn't sleep."

"How did you stop it?"

"I made peace, mostly. My doctor said the trigger was unresolved issues. Things I'd said, done or people I'd hurt, that sort of thing."

"Trin, I refuse to believe you've ever hurt anyone," he said as he smiled. Despite his wild look and sleep deprivation, Anthony had remained a handsome man, somehow retaining his youth and vigour despite his maturity. His dark hair was lightly peppered with grey but his tanned skin was supple and well-maintained.

"Oh I have, sir." She gave a guilty grin and shook her head.

"A heart breaker, I see." He smirked. She looked at him as though it was the first time, not knowing how to react. His behaviour surprised her. She smiled despite herself, looking away awkwardly.

"Come on. We're leaving." She helped him up, resting her shoulder under his underarm, holding his waist as he weakly stumbled along with her. He could barely walk. The weight of his body was a challenge for her small stature but she persisted nonetheless; after all, she had offered to help him and Trin wasn't the type to back out of an offer.

When everybody was ready, Owen asked them to gather around the largest tree in their camp. "We will mark this tree, this time. Right here." Owen took his Swiss army knife from his pocket and carved the roman numeral I in the centre of the trunk. "You all see that I did this and I marked one tree" Everybody nodded on seeing the tree markings. "The next tree I mark will be the numeral for two, then three, then four and so on." Owen turned to Anthony and nodded.

Anthony cleared his throat and addressed the group. "We must not separate. This is an alien world to us. We cannot assume that it's the same as a jungle on Earth, or Atlantis, or New Botswana, or anywhere else. Yesterday, we were naive and the jungle made it clear to us that we do not know what's what around here."

"If we *do* get separated by some means, just stay where you are," Owen added. "Do not eat anything unless you've scanned it first. We really can't afford to lose anyone when there aren't many of us to begin with."

"Sir, I'm not sure what's happened," said Trin, rummaging through her satchel. Her round, freckled face was red.

"What is it?" Owen raised an eyebrow.

"I've lost my compass. It's gone." She looked up at him like a deer in the headlights.

The heaviness in Anthony's gut returned. "Don't worry," he said, forcing a reassuring smile. "If we have a day like yesterday we'll see it again in an hour."

They headed towards the sunrise.

We have to get out of here. If that sun goes down again, I'm a dead man.

Four hours later, the team found themselves at the bottom of a damp, dark hole in the ground.

"It's nothing short of a miracle that we didn't break anything," observed Ade. He had checked on the team in semi-darkness and determined that no bones had been harmed in the drop.

Anthony was furious. He threw his satchel into the darkness with a cry of frustration.

"On the bright side, at least this is different to yesterday," chirped Trin as she retrieved it and brought it back to him. He flushed, having realised what he'd done, and to make matters worse, she acted impervious to his behaviour. "Maybe we did actually get somewhere." She forced a smile. Anthony, having eventually calmed down, switched from fury to embarrassment, paled and received the satchel gratefully.

"Hopefully *somewhere* isn't the local tribe's pitfall trap," said Owen.

Seb looked around. "If this is a trap, I'd hate to see what they're used to catching." The drop was too high for them to reach without a grappling hook. "There's nothing to stand on, either. Not even a few rocks. Fucking hell," Anthony snapped. If there had been a rock nearby, Seb felt that Anthony would have kicked it.

"It's got to be a trap," insisted Trin. "We didn't see it."

"Interesting how it only opened when we were all on it, though." Owen rubbed his chin. "Surely a conventional trap would have buckled with just one of us on it." They looked around with their scanners, measuring the perimeter.

"Owen," Anthony whispered. "It's a snake pit."

"What?" Owen asked impatiently. He looked around their feet and saw nothing but dirt. "There's nothing here."

"It's a snake pit and they're crushing my legs." Anthony started to shake and grabbed Owen's arm.

"Anthony, there are no snakes." Owen, growing concerned, held him fixed and tried to get him to stand up. He looked upon the whites of Anthony's upturned eyes in horror as is friend collapsed with convulsions.

"They're killing me!"

"Anthony, please calm down."

"Help me!" he cried, grabbing Owen by the collar of his shirt. "They're everywhere!" Owen tried to restrain him. The team looked around earnestly but could see nothing. "It's empty!" He was screaming like a madman and writhing in pain. "It burns, it burns. Get them off me!" He jerked as though he was burning at the stake. "It's empty!" he cried once more.

"What's empty?"

"Hell is empty." Owen looked at him to see that he was frothing at the mouth now. Owen felt himself freeze with fear as his friend looked him straight in the eye and for a moment, seemed still and calm. "The Devil, Owen." He immediately returned to jolting with uncontrollable muscle spasms once more. "He's here!" Anthony screamed.

"Ade! Give him a sedative!" instructed Owen as he wrestled with his friend.

Ade obligingly and calmly opened his case and pulled out the sedative. With a quick jab, he pushed it into the side of Anthony's broad neck. Owen and Ade held him down while he cried and threw himself around, thrashing his legs and recoiling. Trin and Seb huddled, looking on helplessly in horror. Trin was crying.

His raw strength finally having left him, he passed out and lay limp on the ground. Owen removed his jacket, rolled it up and dutifully placed it under Anthony's head. He then sat back alongside him and placed his head in his hands.

"Something could have bitten him," Ade suggested, unbuttoning Anthony's shirt and looking for any spots or bites on his torso. He then inspected the length of his arms, around in his ears and across the back of his neck. Nothing.

"This place is driving him mad." Owen glowered up at the hole. "We'll be next." The sun beamed down into the pit, highlighting their lack of exits. It was midday.

Nobody, not even Owen, was willing to acknowledge or talk about the fact that they were ten feet underground in a jungle they had never been to before. They had no map, no compass and no hope of escape.

Silence.

8

A ugust 10, 2300 - eleven years earlier

Every Sunday, those who were forced to call Oceanus 'home' would visit the seaside to observe a day of rest. After having a picnic on the sand dunes, the children would often play on the beach until sundown. On this particular morning, it was just Derrien, Thea and the scientist who had welcomed them to the planet. It was Thea's sixth birthday. Even though her father felt that the offers of birthday excursions or presents were limited on Oceanus, Thea wanted nothing more than a trip to the beach to collect shells.

"Thank you for helping us, Shona," Derrien said whilst they were sitting on the sand dunes overlooking the isolated beach. Hours had passed this way for most of the time that they spent there.

"You would have done the same for me," she smiled with a kindness. "Jet and I are happy that you're here." Her large, doe eyes made her face look friendly and inquisitive no matter the subject. Even when she frowned, Shona never appeared to be serious. Until now.

They looked over to the shoreline where a six year old Thea was beachcombing. She was singing to herself and collecting shells to put in her little net bag.

"Thanks for giving me some work to do here, too. I think I would have gone mad simply sitting around." He feared that he was already going mad and the work was simply delaying his inevitable decline. He found the work dull, tedious and unfulfilling. Sometimes, when digging in the rain, he wanted to storm up to the cottage and demand to be in charge. *Does she know who I am?* She did not know who he was. She didn't seem to care, either.

"Oh that's okay. I understand. A scientist needs their work." She smiled and looked down at the sand, letting her fingers create pits for it to spill into. "I couldn't have you just chopping logs now, could I?" she chuckled.

"I'm not the best botanist, Shona, or the best geologist for that matter."

"I know," she said with a faint smile. "But you'll have to do." They laughed. Derrien's laugh had been more of a forced effort than he could bring himself to admit. He found her infuriating but could not bite the hand that fed him.

Shona had provided them with warm blankets, food, shelter and companionship on the island. For Derrien, she *had* provided some work for him to do to pass the time, even if he felt that she didn't really need him. He dug, collected soil, rocks and various other natural materials. She had never specified what it was that *she* was doing but he buried his mistrust and did the work. No matter how overpowering his curiosity was, he would not look the gift horse in the mouth. *Shona is helping us.*

He had never seen Shona's place of work but respected that if it had been a sensitive project, he had no authority to know the details. He had never had to disclose the details of his own research with his students. As friendly as she was and excellent at small talk, he had never felt that he could ask deeper questions until that day on the beach, two years after they had first met. She seemed more approachable than usual on this day.

"How did you and Jet end up here, alone?" he dared to ask.

Shona took a deep breath and looked away. "Oh, it's a long story, Derrien. Are you sure you want to hear it?" Her face had a unique ability to switch from enthused to tired. She looked wan.

"Not if you don't want to tell me, Shona. I don't want to upset anyone."

"Oh Derrien, you're so kind. Always thinking of others." She laid a hand on his arm.

"I'm glad that you think so. I'm sorry, I've always wondered. How could they just leave you and your son here? It seems barbaric."

He thought of his own circumstances two years before. *How could they?* Had anyone ever bothered to look for the disgraced Professor D. Victor Smith? He had done things that were questionable and felt it was fair enough to stop him in his tracks. But Thea? What had she done to anyone? Did they really deserve to be dispatched into unchartered space to fend for themselves? The heat was rising, bubbling in his blood while he thought about *them. They are murderers. They will pay.*

"The science teams were on a rota to carry out surveys here on Oceanus. We would swap every six months. One day, no one came to relieve me and that was it."

"All these years?"

"Yes. Just Jet and I."

"And no one came to find you?"

"No," she said firmly and looked away again, fidgeting with her dress.

Sensing that she no longer wanted to talk about her arrival on the planet, Derrien reluctantly changed the subject.

"How is Jet?"

"He doesn't say much. He hasn't said much since his father died, really," she sighed. "I just let him express himself in whichever way he can." She gazed into the horizon. "He doesn't have to speak if he doesn't want to."

"When did his father die, if you don't mind me asking?"

"Just after we arrived here, he killed himself. Jet was four years old."

"Shona, I'm so sorry."

"He didn't sleep, hardly ate, and walked the breadth of the island most nights. I hardly knew him any more. He jumped off that cliff there." She pointed to one of the sea cliffs to the west of where they were sitting. "It's ok Derrien," she said, looking at her friend's shocked face. "It was a long time ago."

"I lost my wife, too," he said quietly.

"Oh, I'm so sorry."

"Thea barely knew her." His eyes filled up with tears but they could not come. He swallowed and fought them back, taking a deep breath.

"We don't have to talk if you don't want to," she said quietly.

The pair sat and watched Thea happily at work for a short while. She looked up, waved and returned to her beachcombing. The sun was beating down on them by now and the clouds had been burned away. The tide had departed and left ample room for the seabirds to start their hunt for gifts that the waves had left behind.

"It's a shame they did drop offs and didn't leave you with a means of escape, especially with…" Derrien bowed his head, thinking of the man who had taken his own life many years before. "It's an alien world, after all."

"It is."

"Rather an oversight, in my opinion." He sensed his pulse beginning to race as he risked the comment. Shona did not entertain it.

There must be a bloody ship, Shona. What are you hiding from me? No reputable scientific research organisation would leave a team member out here, not to mention one who clearly has a family with her. How much longer do I have to eat this?

Instead she stood up and stretched like a cat after a long nap under a warm window. "Shall we go for a walk?" she asked, hands on hips.

Despite his frustration from never having had a clear answer from Dr Lennox about most things to do with the obscure planet, Derrien was grateful for the friendship and agreed to go with her. "Thea, we're going for a walk," he said, waving to his child. She obligingly skipped along behind them.

Up over the sand dunes was a slightly wooded path to the centre of the island. Birds darted up and over the sandy hills and brought with them their shrill calls. Rabbits and red squirrels shot past the path to sit elsewhere and watch, their large black eyes opening and closing. The tufts of dry grass susurrated in the firing line of the sea breeze as Shona and Derrien strolled along the dusty walkway.

He had been this way many, many times before. The beach stayed the same. The coastal path stayed the same. How many more years could Derrien endure the same? He wondered. He looked over at his little girl. She had once known Atlantis, a temperate world, not much different to this one, only bigger, all the conveniences of modern technology and with more people. More faces to look at. Thea was born in the year 2294. At the time, both her mother and father were highly praised for their work on advanced cyber and AI defence technology. "To defeat it, you have to understand it," Derrien would say to his students at the University to great applause. "Enemies are defeated when we truly know them."

He remembered the day he met Thea's mother, Cara Tate. A tall, red haired lady ten years older than he was, she was both beautiful and a genius; an intimidating mix for an average man. Lucky for Derrien, average was never a word his peers would apply to his character.

"I've never seen anything like this. I feel like the grey lady from earth," she joked, looking down at her beige raincoat and brown trousers and taking in the beauty and blueness of the colony. The light on the water dazzled like diamonds with every crest of wave. They were standing at a sea view window on campus, basking in the warmth of that summer's day.

As far as Derrien was concerned, Venus had arrived at Atlantis, her hair flowing and angels rushing in to adorn her in silks but she did not need the assistance of any angels. She was adorned by her charm, her wit and her intelligence. For the first time in his academic career, Derrien loved something more than his work.

She had first met him when supervising his PhD at the University. The day after his PhD was awarded, they married in a private, civil ceremony on the island of Nafplion.

They did not know about the tumour, then.

They would not know about the cancer until Thea was two years old. In spite of man's technological and medical advances in previous centuries, new, rare and poorly researched brain cancers remained the most deadly and problematic of all.

She died in her husband's arms in a hospice by the sea, aged forty-eight.

With an all consuming feeling of emptiness, Derrien looked out at the sand dunes now as he had done then. He had known Cara for five years. Sometimes, in his darker moods, he thought that loving Cara had been a moment's pleasure in exchange for a lifetime of pain. She may have been the love of his life but she had also been the catalyst in his downfall.

On Oceanus, various grasses and wildflowers grew as Derrien had found when sampling the local flora for Shona. He was not particularly enamoured with becoming a makeshift botanist but he found the work fulfilling for the time being.

This spot had also become a favourite play area for his daughter. Daddy's work was boring but flowers were always interesting for a child. Thea, true to form, skipped around looking for daisies while the adults stopped to wait. Derrien, intrigued by the revelation of a deceased Mr Lennox, looked west of their direction. There was nothing there. No stones, cross or cairn in sight.

Perhaps she didn't want little Jet coming to a windy cliff edge to visit Dad. Fair enough. Maybe they have something at home instead.

A windswept Shona raised her hand over her eyes to shield them from the sun as she peered into the distance. "It's Jet," she remarked happily.

Across the way, emerging from the wood that surrounded Shona's cottage was a skinny, dark haired boy of the age of seven or eight wearing handmade rag clothes. He wore a solemn, permanent sulk as he walked towards them, carrying something in his hand.

"Has he caught a rabbit?" asked Derrien.

Jet approached and ran past the adults to find Thea. He stopped abruptly and held out the object.

"Is this for me?" the little girl asked. The barefooted boy, bashful and mute as always, simply nodded. She took it from him and held it to her chest.

"Thank you," she beamed. "Daddy! Daddy! Look!" She rushed to Derrien and held it up. It was a rag doll made out of old pieces of cloth. Its hair had been painted red just like Thea's.

"Happy Birthday, Thea," said Shona, smiling down at the little girl.

***

Present Day

Journal of D Victor Smith - November 2, 2311

If only he'd read those damn journals. J is as stubborn as I am which leaves us at this stalemate of sorts. If he'd just fucking read them, we'd be in a better place. I did what I had to do.

We have to get off this planet. But what about the others? What will become of them? I have no control over it. It's not me. It's that thing. It won't let me fucking sleep. It grips me like opium and I can't shake it off. It hurt him. He hates my guts but that was new. Didn't like it.

Ship seems to be in good working order. Only carries four. Could have been the four of us all those fucking years ago. I can't leave those people behind. I hate you, Shona Lennox.

9

— · —

You may never know what results come of your actions, but if you do nothing, there will be no results.

Balthazar stared at the Mahatma Ghandi quote on his desktop screensaver for a few minutes before opening his computer. What was he hoping to achieve? Save the crew? From where? He didn't even know where they were. He *hoped* that they were on that little wet planet down there.

Hours passed with little to no progress. Balthazar switched his computer off and went to bed.

That night, he dreamed.

"Balths, excellent work!" His father greeted him in the doorway of his cabin. Hamza Swain was wearing his favourite dinner suit. "Hurry up now, we can't be late!" Hamza tapped his vintage wristwatch and put his hands in his pockets.

"Late for what?" asked the bleary-eyed Balthazar.

"Ha! Balths, always the joker." Hamza turned away and headed down the corridor. Balthazar followed him to a large conference hall adorned with white-clothed tables and huge velvet curtains. People were talking and laughing, wearing their finest evening attire. His father walked over to a table in the centre of the room where his mother, Priya, was sitting enjoying a martini.

"Balthazar, darling!" She smiled her usual warm, encouraging smile and raised her glass to him. "You made mama proud tonight." She was wearing diamonds in her wavy black hair. She looked like a Queen of Persia, sitting in a sea of floating lights.

"Proud? What's going on?" His anxiety was growing again. He was as nervous as he usually was when his mother was happy about something. Had he been signed up to singing lessons, tennis, amateur dramatics? He wanted to know why his mother was so happy.

Priya Swain was a loving mother, a listener and a diplomat but she was seldom proud of Balthazar's behaviour.

When Balthazar was twelve, he stuttered and bumbled through his first performance as Hamlet. He died inside, several times to the sound of coughing and chair scraping. "I want you to be the best," his mother would say on the way into the am dram. "Your grandfather was a fine actor."

When he was thirteen, he scored not one but three own goals for his team. Priya had suggested that "sport is great for making new friends." But those friends would not want to be on the same team ever again.

Now, at twenty, Balthazar was still that anxious, shaking mess that felt he had disappointed his parents at every turn.

He was perplexed. The people were seated now, falling silent as admiral James Winter took to the stage and addressed them all through the microphone.

Where am I?

"Thank you for coming here tonight," he said in his gruff, Scottish accent. "It's an honour to be here and even more of an honour to present this award to Mr Balthazar Swaine."

Oh my God.

The room erupted into applause and cheers. Balthazar floated over to the stage. Admiral Winter smiled at him earnestly and held out a large, strong hand to shake. His white beard had been trimmed for the occasion and he seemed to have fewer laugh lines than Balthazar had remembered. A giant of a man, he bent over dramatically to drape a medal over Balthazar's head, like a headmaster awarding prizes on junior school sports day.

I want to get off now.

"Thank you," Balthazar said calmly. He turned to face the audience who were clapping again. His mother sparkled in the stage lights, wiping tears from her eyes with a giant white handkerchief.

Say something. Say something cool.

He said nothing and slunk away from the stage, returning to his parents.

After a few rounds of awards for various other things that Balthzar couldn't quite hear or understand, people were invited to the dining room. He followed the crowd as they rambled into a great, high-ceilinged room with decorative marble columns and buttresses. It had the grandeur of a cathedral but there were no relics, paintings, stained glass windows or pews. Instead, it had floor-to-ceiling windows and thousands of lights dangling from ornate chandeliers.

Tables, covered in a similar way to the tables in the other room, were arranged neatly across the shiny, marbled floor, like a wedding reception.

Somehow, Balthazar was seated next to an old school friend, Dev Khan. Dev was a tall, bird-like engineering student he had known on Mars as a teenager. Unlike Balthazar, Dev was in the top set for everything and excelled at all sports. He was handsome, charismatic, successful and smart. Always smart. Balthazar, as much as he enjoyed hanging out with Dev sometimes, really despised him now. He despised him even more tonight as he sat looking like India's answer to James Bond.

Fuck you, Dev.

In contrast to the dashing, black-tied Dev, Balthazar was short and dumpy with a permanent expression of surprise. He couldn't help it. His eyebrows had always been shaped like that: bushy and raised too far above his eyes.

"Really sorry to hear about your condition, mate," Dev leaned in and said quietly with a little elbow jab. He gave Balthazar a kind smile.

"Condition?"

"Yeah. Devastating. I think about you most days, mate." Dev took a sip of his wine and looked out into the distance.

Balthazar wasn't sure that he knew what his school friend was talking about. He tried to ask but the words would not come. Then the waiting staff brought the first course to the tables.

The serving staff laid the plates down onto their table and Dev immediately covered his mouth in shock. He looked at Balthazar and erupted into hysterical laughter, as did the woman next to him and eventually, all of the table. The laughter spread like wildfire across the dining room. Everybody was looking at him.

Balthazar glanced downward at the dish and saw two sui mai that had been painted in a radioactive green food colouring. Why this was funny, he didn't know but his instinct was to recoil in shame. He swiftly left the room and headed back to his cabin, unable to think of anything other than the green sui mai.

He burst in and removed his jacket in a desperate attempt to cool down. He wanted to wake up. He couldn't wake up. He tried splashing his face with cold water in the basin but nothing happened. He stopped for a moment, leaning over the vanity and staring at his reflection.

Why was it green?

"Balthazar." He heard his father's voice again. Hamza was standing in the doorway as he had before the awards ceremony.

"Dad, what's my condition?" Balthazar asked in panic. Hamza's eyebrows lowered in a look of pity and he cast a look down at Balthazar's crotch.

"I'll be outside," he said quietly. The hydraulic door, hissing and clunking, closed behind him with a click.

Balthazar untied his belt and looked down at his crotch. His stomach dropped.

Somehow, somewhere, Balthazar had become the owner of a radioactive green scrotum.

"The fuck?" he screeched. "No, no, no." Pacing across his cabin, he could say nothing other than, "No, no, no." for a time. He banged his fist against the wall in despair. "This isn't happening." He started to cry. "Dad!" His voice broke as he called out for him. No answer. "Dad!" Still no answer. He rushed to the door and opened it. There was nobody there. The corridor was as empty as it had been on the first night he found himself alone. He peered down again and saw that his scrotum was the expected colour and as unexciting as ever. He sighed with relief. *It was just a weird dream.*

He had fallen asleep while working at his computer again. The database query was still sitting at "Autopilot guide".

He resolved to try his luck on the bridge.

Having no experience of flying a space vessel, or any vessel for that matter, the controls on the bridge of the Demeter were a mystery to Balthazar Swaine. He had spent hours upon hours poring over the pages of various manuals and databases while there. He decided to try and speak with the ship's computer system, Liana, again.

"Please select a destination," Liana's voice instructed.

"Yes! Get in." Balthazar rubbed his hands together.

"We could not find that destination. Please try again."

"Atlantis," he said clearly.

"Atlantic Ocean. Earth."

"No, no."

"Do you want to proceed?"

"No."

"Request cancelled." The screen blackened with a negative sound-ing "duh-dum."It had switched itself off. Balthazar switched it back on and waited for the intro jingle to run its course.

"Please select a destination." Liana sounded jolly this time, adopt-ing the enthusiasm of a tour guide Barbie doll, fresh out of the box.

"AHT-LAN-TIS."

"Atlantis. Atlantis."

"Yes."

"Please select the origin."

I have no idea. Balthazar tried to select the option for "Find my location." but he was met with "error."

"Find my location, please." He tried speaking to the computer this time.

"I'm sorry. Location cannot be found. Please input your location."

"Oh shitting hell."

"Do you mean Shitterton, UK, Earth?"

"No! Cancel request."

"Request cancelled."

"I don't know the location."

"Please enter coordinates."

"I don't know the coordinates."

"I'm sorry. Autopilot requires the origin in order to map the jour-ney."

I don't know where I am. Balthazar shut the computer off.

He returned to his cabin, despondent and tired. Laying on his bed, he thought for a while and repeatedly threw and caught a cricket ball in the air. Hamza had been an excellent cricketer. Despite Hamza's fatherly, unbounded encouragement, Balthazar could not bat. He could catch though. There was that at least.

There was a knock on the door which caused him to look away from the ball for a moment. Thump. The ball smacked him directly on the right cheekbone, stinging the surrounding area in a blinding fury and bringing a tear to his eye.

Balthazar, you idiot. Answer the door.

Balthazar jolted up and sat on the edge of the bed. It was gentle knocking, as though late at night. He looked at his clock. It was only three p.m in the afternoon. The knocking continued, slowly but surely.

"Balthazar, are you there?" It was a woman's voice in a hushed tone. He quickly looked in his mirror and slicked his black hair back then checked his breath in his hands. Opening the door, he looked up in a mix of fright and pleasant surprise.

Standing outside the door was an incredibly tall, striking blonde woman with long, golden hair. She was wearing a blue mini dress with a matching pillbox hat. Her curved, full lips were painted pink and she had dramatically long, black eyelashes. *Like barbie.*

"Why didn't you let me in?" she smiled. Her teeth were perfectly straight and almost glowing white. She spoke with a sweet, American accent, momentarily transporting him to somewhere in the deep American south, just like in the films.

"There's no one else here. I thought..."

"Thought you were all alone?" She giggled and covered her mouth with her pretty long fingers. Her nails had been painted pink to match her lips. "You're so funny."

"What is happening?" He asked in bewilderment. She tottered past him in ridiculously high, pink stilettos and sat down on the bed.

"It's me, silly."

He panicked. Had he been on a date with this woman and forgot to call? Was she the girl he had abandoned in the bar a month ago because he'd accidentally punched himself in the face when a party trick went horribly wrong and had to find a way to get rid of the blood in his mouth? He wasn't sure he'd ever seen her before but at the same time, she was familiar to him. She had noticed that he was looking at her strangely and tittered. "It's me! Liana."

"Liana?"

"Yeah. Liana, honey." Her accent had relaxed into something that sounded like a sweet, silvery tinkle akin to that of Dolly Parton.

"Liana?" he asked again, processing the name.

The computer. Liana is the computer.

"Yeah! It's me!" She smiled and laughed, shaking her head. "You're so silly, you Martian boys."

"Right." He laughed nervously, still standing in the doorway. She was twirling her long hair around her fingers and smiling at him. Her long, tanned legs were crossed now. He made an effort to close his mouth. "Don't gawk," his mother would say. She was saying it now in his head.

"Are you lost, baby?"

Baby? Are we a thing now?

"Actually, yes. I don't know where I am."

"Aw Balthazar, come here," she said in a sympathetic voice with her arms outstretched. He did not want to move but he felt compelled to. He sat beside her on the bed. She was so warm and welcoming. He was so lost and alone.

"That little planet down there? That's called *Oceanus*." She pointed to the floor of the cabin. "Make sure you put it in your next message. Maybe they'll reply."

"Oceanus?" He shrugged. "I've never heard of it."

"Not many people have, honey. It's a secret." She placed a finger on her lips and shushed gently.

"A secret? Why?"

"Oh, I can't tell you that." She shook her head cheekily and batted her dramatic, feline eyelashes at him. "But you just go on ahead and tell them that's where you are." She placed her hands on his chest and tenderly started unfastening the buttons of his shirt. This made him jump back and remove her hands.

"Ok. I'd better go then!"

"I didn't mean right now." She laughed. "What about lil ol' me?" She pouted, folding her arms.

"Sorry. Erm, maybe later." He backed out of the cabin, crashing into everything in his blinded path and ran back to the bridge.

10

— · —

For almost twenty years, a small research launch, Galileo, remained hidden inside a hangar within the western cliffs of Oceanus, never to be used again. Commissioned by the Interplanetary Science Council in 2091, the vessel had been vital in supporting planetary research across the sector. It waited, mothballed with its nose to the camouflage doors of the hangar.

No one on Oceanus knew about its existence. No one, except for Derrien Victor Smith.

Derrien had decided that no one would ever know about it, either. With the axe that he had carried from the woodshed, he approached the vessel. What stopped him from taking the first swing was not the enormity of the vessel in comparison to his human dimensions but a force that he couldn't identify. He tried again to lift the axe; his arms were pushed back as though the ship itself was the repelling side of the magnet.

"Derrien..." a woman's voice said softly. He gasped and held his breath. He tried not to see her form in the far right corner of the hangar– a darker grey against rock. His heart was thudding in his ears. The grey, dullness of the concrete and her shadowed shape merged in his peripheral vision at first. He closed his eyes and shook his head, opening them again and looking to his left and then to his right. There was nobody there. He was imagining things, he was sure of it. Shona Lennox was long dead.

"Derrien…" the voice said again. It was in his ear and at the same time, echoing around the hangar, bouncing off the high walls. His vision blurred and his ears buzzed for a moment. He shook his head.

He tried to attack the ship again. His arms were forced away again and again each time he started afresh. "No!" he cried, his veins throbbing in his temples.

"Put it down, Derrien." The voice was closer now. It was calm, disarming. It was Shona Lennox's voice. "Derrien. You cannot ignore me," she said. He bowed his head in defeat. "It goes into *space*, Derrien. The hull can handle up to 10,000 degrees and you're coming at it with an axe? Come on, put it down."

"You're not real."

"Derrien, listen to me."

"No, no no no." Derrien dropped the axe and began to slap his head. "No, no no."

"Derrien, stop that." He felt her hand touch his arm. It was the same hand he had known all those years ago. The shock of her presence vibrated through his body and made the hairs on the back of his neck stand to attention. He felt cold. "Put it down."

"You're not real," he sobbed. "You can't be."

"I am. Derrien, I am here." She smiled with her friendly, wide smile. Her eyes were creased either side with laugh lines. They were her eyes.

Shona Octavia Lennox, his former mentor and friend, stood before him in the hangar. When she looked up at him, her large brown eyes penetrated and touched what little was left of his soul.

"Shona?" he asked. He rubbed his eyes.

"It's me, Derrien." She held out a hand and touched his cheek. Her hand felt as real as Thea's hand or Geraint's hand. He was sure that

Jet's hand would have felt real too, had he ever felt it. Derrien's bottom lip trembled as he tried to speak to her.

"Do you want to tell me what's going on?" she asked with a smirk as she looked up at the ship. "Just what were you doing to my ship with that tiny, flimsy axe?"

He crumpled into her arms and wept like a child, taking deep, guttural breaths. She held him there, gently shushing and stroking his head. After a time, he calmed down.

"I have to destroy it, Shona. They can't get away." He pulled away from her, holding back any further tears. She looked at his blotchy skin and reddened eyes with sympathy.

"Who can't get away?" she frowned.

"Anthony, Owen... The rest of them." His voice was laced with contempt. She studied him as he paced the floor cursing them. "They all deserve to die."

"What about those you care about?"

"Thea isn't going anywhere. She's safe here," he snapped.

"And what about Jet? What about my boy, Derrien?"

Her boy. Derrien looked away. He had not thought of Jet since the incident the day before. Jet had the same, piercing eyes as his mother. They also shared thick, straight black hair and olive skin. He could barely look at Shona without seeing the young man who had been beside himself with rage just a day ago.

"Derrien, look at me."

He did as he was told. "It has to be this way, Shona." He looked away again.

"Does it?" She eyed him as if searching desperately, trying to find the man she once knew. His eyes were heavy, troubled and plagued with an eternal sadness; he wore deep worry lines across his face.

"They must pay. They *must.*" He felt his temper rising.

"What your brother did..." she began, calmly, "was–"

"Was a crime, Shona!"

"And what you did wasn't?" She raised an eyebrow.

Shona always knew where to hit Derrien hard. His mouth opened but no words followed. He sat down on the floor and hugged his knees. She knelt beside him and put her arm around him. "An eye for an eye, Derrien. It leaves all of us blind."

"What have I done?"

"You sought revenge. It's a perfectly normal response."

"But to kill them, Shona? Am I capable of that?"

"You're really asking me this, aren't you?"

Derrien felt the air rapidly leave his lungs. Her words had punched him in the stomach. He was a murderer. He had never accepted it until now. "Shona, I—"

"Just kidding Derrien. I know I deserved it." She gave him a nudge with her elbow.

He twiddled his fingers like a child struggling to find the right words. "Shona. I—"

"Honestly, I understand. What I did was horrible. You did what you had to do." She stood up and put her hands in her pockets. "What are you doing to them anyway? Just having a bit of fun?"

"I'd hardly call it fun. I feel terrible about it but at the same time, I can't stop myself."

Shona took a deep breath. "What they did to you *was* wrong but we both know that two wrongs don't make a right." She laughed at herself. "Sorry, I had to get in there with another proverb, didn't I?"

"You did." He nodded with a faint smile.

Derrien stood up again and looked up at the spacecraft parked in the hangar. "Maybe they can go home. Maybe I should go home. Who knows?"

"You don't have to decide right now." She stepped back and admired the vessel. "I wonder if she still fires up."

He shook his head. "I can't, Shona."

"Maybe not today then, but you do need to get off this planet, Derrien." She fixed her gaze directly in his sad, grey eyes again. "Jet needs to get off this planet."

Neither of them spoke for a few moments. Derrien, lost in thought, stared at the ship. It had been maintained by Shona and he had carried the torch in her absence. The ship could leave that day, if Derrien wished it.

"You know I did what I had to do, don't you?" he asked sheepishly.

"I do."

"Do you forgive me?"

"Of course I do. I was wrong."

"You were wrong about *that*, yes, but you were right about the other thing."

"I was? That's terrible."

"I tried to–"

"I know but we should forget about that now. We need to save them, Derrien. I don't know how much time we have left."

"Days, if that."

"Come on then. Hop to it." She nodded towards the secret entrance.

"Shona, I've missed you." Derrien said as he walked away.

"I've missed you too."

He turned to give her one final glance and, realising that he was alone again, left the hangar.

11

— · —

Geraint, feeling tiredness finally setting in, sat down on some rocks that lay between the woods and the path back to the cottage. After exploring the long, isolated beach and the coastal path from the sand dunes with Thea, he had had enough of Oceanus. He hated it. It was miserable, filling him with an inescapable sense of despair everywhere he looked.

He watched the red squirrels scurry past and clamber up and down the lonely trees, rummaging and then subsequently burying their treasures. Rabbits hopped past in the distance and disappeared for a time, only to resurface again and bounce to the other side of the meadow.

This was nothing like home. He felt that it had a coldness to it, whereas Atlantis was always warm. This place was wild and windy. Atlantis was calm. His family was there. His mother was there. What was she doing right then at that moment? Was she worried for him? What were his sisters doing? He felt his stomach churn at the prospect of them grieving for him. A notice would be sent around the next of kin. Lost in space. A death sentence.

Perhaps he'd return long after they'd gone. No one knew how these stories ended. With the expansion of space exploration came risk of uncharted anomalies and hostile territory. He was dead as far as anybody outside of Oceanus was concerned. Ships vanished all the time.

In spite of his thoughts about his family, he believed that his father was still alive.

I am alive. Why shouldn't he be?

His thoughts were interrupted by the shrill calls of the sand martins. They soared and dived and disappeared together. The harsh wind was calmer on this particular afternoon. The weak warmth of the sun cast its light on the coastal path and the dry clusters of tall grass.

Thea was still standing, looking back towards the sea. "I've always loved the water," she remarked. "It's always been the same." She had been collecting some daisies and placing them in her pocket. She saw him looking and winked. "They make good dye, you know."

Thea was the only thing he liked about this place. She was always smiling, always fascinated by the nature around her. He couldn't bear to think of her as a simpleton. He wanted to believe that this was what *good natured* was. Not every action had to be clever, ambitious or calculated. She was beautiful to him again. He wanted to stay with her, but not on Oceanus. She was his only friend in the world at that moment, no matter how baffling she was.

"Would you leave here?" Geraint asked. Thea seemed surprised by his question. What he wanted to ask was *would you come with me*?

"Leave?" she pondered. "I've never thought about it."

"Have you never felt bored of this place?" he asked, casually tossing a pebble.

"Not really." She smiled and sat down beside Geraint, placing her hands on her knees. "This has always been a home to me. I don't know why but I feel I could never leave." She shuddered at the thought.

There it was. The rejection had been served, cold and lumpy and in want of a spoon. If she didn't want to leave, it meant she didn't want to come with *him*. Fighting the urge to give a knee jerk reaction, he swallowed his pride and raised an eyebrow. "Even though there's not much here?"

"There's not much here, no. It's home though," she said coyly.

"But it's just you and your Dad," he remarked. "And that other guy." He had never seen the elusive Jet but accepted that he existed, somewhere. "Don't you worry about being lonely one day?"

"No. I have my father. That's all I need."

Derrien Victor Smith. Something Geraint couldn't quite grasp was the girl's dependence on her father. He had seemed like a madman. Why didn't she want to get away and see the worlds out there? It was unfathomable to him. He thought of all the times where he couldn't wait to get out on his own. Remembering his last voyage, he felt terrible for acting unenthused about accompanying his father to New Botswana. He missed his father more than he ever had before.

"But you're seventeen, Thea. You should get out and see the galaxy."

She didn't respond. She instead stared into the distance, watching the rabbits hop from burrow to burrow. He felt sick with disappointment. "I first went out when I was five. It wasn't scary. There were loads of things to do and see. You just get used to it." He smiled at her as she turned her towards him. She smiled back.

"Do you?"

Geraint nodded and took a deep breath. "Maybe you could come and see it... s-see it with me?" He leaned forward and stretched out a hand. She didn't take it.

A silence opened between them and she looked away with an emptiness in her eyes. He saw that she was crying and panicked. The air felt cold suddenly, causing him to shiver in his light shirt.

"I'm sorry. I didn't mean to upset you." Geraint placed his hand on her back and rubbed it, not knowing what else to do. She continued to sob into her hands.

"I can never leave here. I don't know why. I can't even think about it." Her tears fell fast now. "I just couldn't." Geraint embraced her and stroked her long, wavy hair. "It's not that I don't like you, I do." She tried to slow her breathing but the tears were uncontrollable. "I'm trapped here. You don't understand. You couldn't."

"I'm sorry," he whispered. "I didn't mean to make you cry." He discovered that he hated seeing her cry. "Why are you trapped? Is it your father?"

She gently pushed away from him, shook her head and wiped her eyes. "I'm sorry. I can't talk about this right now. I should go. I'll see you at the cottage." She gestured for him to stay seated and pointed towards the thicker part of the woodland in the distance. "It's through there." She left him there alone to watch her shape grow smaller and smaller until it disappeared into the trees.

With a sigh, Geraint turned his back and looked around. Noticing that there were several more rocks behind him, he decided to follow their trail. Thea leaving him behind gave him licence to do whatever he wanted, he felt.

What's up there anyway? he thought with a scowl, expecting there to be nothing but more rabbits and maybe a sparrowhawk or a falcon. The trees had shed their leaves more vigorously up on the cliffs. Their bare branches held off the sea breeze as well as they could. The trees, he supposed, had been pummelled by the extreme winds so much so that they had succumbed to pressure that twisted them into gnarled sentries overlooking the wastes below. The rocky path that they guarded was bare. No grass grew here: just dirt, sand, and shadow.

He had already decided that this island was awful but Thea hadn't said anything about predators or poisons. Perhaps there were none. He had been stung by a small, white scorpion once on Atlantis as a boy. Not much came of it as their hospitals were well equipped with antidotes and antihistamines. If a scorpion were to sting him here, he wasn't sure what the outcome would be. Derrien wouldn't save him. Thea would save him if Derrien allowed it. He felt himself growing resentful of them both. Both had been difficult when he had asked for assistance finding his father. He resolved to track Owen down by himself. He also vowed to himself that he wouldn't return to the cottage that night or ever.

Geraint had followed the stones to the cliffs of the island that stood overlooking the sea. The cool breeze ruffled his dark brown hair and took his breath away. He looked around, admiring the view of the dramatic albeit savage landscape. He was at the highest peak of the island, where a sparse carpet of grass and flowers had sprung up in defiance of the elements. *I'm king of this island*. He smiled to himself and shook his head.

Behind him, to the east, were the sand dunes, the beach and the walkway back to the woods which he had learned lay in the centre of the island. West and south of him was nothing but vast, black ocean and grey skies. He would go north, where there seemed to be a mass of jungle covered with low clouds. *A wood and a jungle*. He had never seen a combination like that before.

A pang of trepidation settled into his stomach as he thought about his plan. *What if I get lost?*

"What's the worst case scenario?" He heard his father's voice in his head.

"I have to go back to the start," was his answer. He sat down for a moment on a patch of grass and regarded the daisies around him.

They stared up at him with happy yellow faces and white petals. A bright, white, bridal trail of them guided his eyes to more stones that grew dramatically in numbers until they reached a grand mound. It was a cairn. Someone had been buried there. Geraint walked over to investigate further.

On the cairn lay a little cluster of rags. He crouched for a closer look and reached for it.

In his hands he held a weather worn shape made of cloth, stuffed with fabric and feathers. It was sunbleached and washed out but he could make out the remains of what had once been a child's doll.

12

—·—

In a small woodcutter's hut on the southern edge of the lake, Jet lived alone. It was a single room lodging with a humble kitchenette, some books stacked on a single shelf and a bed with a small table beside it. On the far side of the room was a small fireplace and one wooden chair. The only clue as to the identity of the person who lived there was the small table by the bed where there stood a framed photograph of Shona Lennox.

He had come to live there as a boy, after the death of his mother. Barely fourteen, he isolated himself from Derrien as quickly as he could.

Jet was lying on his bed listening to the erratic pitter-patter of rain when there was a knock at the door. He recognised it instantly but did not move despite the overwhelming compulsion to dart out of bed and open it. He did not feel like talking right now, not even to a friend.

The knocking persisted. "Jet, I know you're in there." Jet, alarmed to hear that she sounded upset, straightened. The sound of her voice, much to his annoyance at being disturbed, dissipated his anger. He went to the door and unbolted it without further question.

Even in the heavy downpour, the girl was a sight to behold. Thea stood there in the rain, her hair drenched and pin-straight. The droplets rolling down her forehead and cheeks disguised her tears well.

The small breaths and quivering in her voice told him all he needed to know. He moved aside and let her in.

She removed her wet shawl from her shoulders and wiped her eyes. "I have nowhere else to go, Jet."

"What? You live in the—"

"No," she shook her head vehemently, "I don't live there any more."

Jet closed the door and returned to the bed where he sat down. Thea did not sit down with him. She paced the small room, stopping to admire the small collection of books. Jet had a copy of Robinson Crusoe that she had read multiple times as well as a vintage Shakespeare anthology and several collections of poetry. For a boy who hardly spoke, he was as well read as could be on their little island.

She looked tired. More tired than he had ever seen her. Her smiling disposition was nowhere to be seen. He studied her as she fidgeted with the books. "I don't know what's happened to me but I'm not myself," she finally said as she flicked through a copy of Sylvia Plath's collected poems. "Something has changed. I feel different."

"The new boy?" Jet asked, folding his arms. He had spied Geraint through a chink in the garden wall the previous morning and had surprised himself with his own jealousy. It consumed him, nagging at him in the back of his mind ever since.

"No. Nothing to do with Geraint. It's *me*."

"What's wrong with you?"

"I don't know. I don't understand."

"Does your father know?"

"No. I don't want to tell him either."

Jet didn't know what to say. Most of his frustrations with Thea stemmed from her unwavering loyalty to her father. At first, he saw it as no different to any child's bond with a parent but as they grew older, he kept his distance from her, at least when it came to emotions. The sudden change in behaviour was disconcerting. He decided to tread lightly.

"I was at the beach with Geraint," she began, "and he asked me about leaving the planet. I said I couldn't possibly do that. It just wasn't an option." She sat down in the chair and twiddled her fingers. "I realised then that I'd never thought about it before," she said, staring at the fire. "I've never thought beyond existing. I suppose I tend to my garden but my life has been about serving my father." She twisted her long hair in her hands and wrung it. "I've never thought about my own life. I've just existed. Isn't that funny?"

Jet could find nothing to say. He watched with his mouth agape for what felt like an eternity and finally pinned something down. "Did Geraint ask you to go with him?"

"Yes. I said I couldn't do it and I didn't know why."

"Well, we don't have any transport," he remarked. "Is that what you mean?"

"No. I mean I had never thought beyond my life here."

Her words saddened him. For as long as he could remember, he dreamed of escaping Oceanus. His mother had promised him that they'd return home soon but 'soon' had become five years, ten years and eventually, never. Still, he had not given up hope.

"I have never thought about leaving here. When he asked me, I said it wasn't possible but I don't know why. I just know that it isn't."

"Don't talk like that. There's a–"

"No. For *you* there may be. It's not for me. I know it in my heart." Thea rose and quickly put some more firewood into the fire. She sat down again in the chair, half looking at him. "When I had that conversation today, it made me feel so uncomfortable. I wanted to run. I didn't understand why."

"Perhaps you do want to leave."

"I think it's more than that," she said. "Something keeps me here."

"Your father?"

"That's the funny thing, Jet. It's not him. I'm free of him now."

"What do you mean?"

"I mean I felt absolutely no compulsion to return home or to tell *him* any of this," she said, looking at Jet. "I wanted to tell you and that's what I did."

"He didn't tell you to?"

"No. I wanted to come here." She smiled for the first time that evening. "I *wanted* to come here." Her large blue eyes met his. "Do you know what any of this means?" she asked him. He looked away.

"Only you know your own mind, Thea."

"I don't, though." For the first time, she said something to him that sounded angry. "I've never thought before," she said, "I didn't think about anything, really. I just did everything I was asked. Today, I really thought about my life and I came to the horrifying realisation that my father is a monster. He has done terrible things and I stand by and do nothing because I could *only* do nothing. I had no say because I gave no thought."

"Do nothing about what?"

"Everything, Jet. The way he treats me. The things he has done to people. The way he treats... you." Her voice broke, "I can't bear it."

Jet looked at the photograph on his bedside table. His mother was looking back at him with a smile. The anger in his heart rose up again. He wanted to kill Derrien Victor Smith.

Thea turned to look at him. "We're all going to die here." Her eyes filled up with tears again. She bit her bottom lip and swallowed, "we'll all die here because *he* wills it so." Jet rose from the bed and hugged her tightly.

"We don't have to die here," he said softly. She sobbed into his shoulder. As much as it frightened him to see her cry, his instincts overwhelmed him. "There's always a way, Thea. We can get out of here."

She looked up at him and smiled faintly. "You think so?"

"Yes. I won't let anything happen to you, I promise." His arms were still around her.

"Jet," she asked, "can I kiss you?"

He was taken aback at her request. "What?"

"Can I kiss you?"

"Is this some kind of joke?"

"No. I need to know something and I won't know unless I kiss you."

"Ok."

She kissed him. Against his better judgement, he passionately reciprocated until she changed her mind and pulled away. She unpicked his fingers from her body like the love-starved barnacles she'd found on a rowboat.

"It's no good," she protested.

"What's no good?" He leaned in again. She dodged his attempt, holding her hands up to block him.

"It doesn't work."

It felt like a punch in the gut. His breath had abandoned him. "What do you mean?" he asked, crestfallen.

"I feel nothing when I kiss you," she said, looking him in the eye. "I just..." she thought for a moment as he stared at her, incredulously, waiting for her to ease the pain with *sorry, I didn't mean it*. "I just had to know, Jet," she continued, sitting down on the bed. "Geraint kissed me in the garden and I didn't understand why," she admitted.

"I asked him why and he didn't tell me. I thought by kissing you, I'd understand better but I'm just as confused as I was before."

"I'm confused, too," Jet said with knotted eyebrows. He wanted the confusion to be over. He wanted her to go away and leave him to lick his wounds.

"I don't have any feelings. That's another thing I've realised." she announced.

"Why are you crying, then?"

She hadn't noticed the fresh tears rolling down her face until now. She *was* crying. He looked at her pitifully. "I don't think you know what you're saying," he said softly, wiping her tears away. She pulled away from him once more.

"You mean, I don't know my own mind?" she asked with a hint of accusation.

Jet was amazed at her new found assertiveness, "no, I just mean... you're confused," he shrugged. "Also, you *did* come in here and tell me you don't know who you are any more so yes, forgive me for thinking you're confused." He waved his hands in exasperation and sat down on the bed again.

"Don't tell me what I think, Jet. I've had enough of that all my life."

She seemed small to him now. Vulnerable. He let go of his resentment and sighed. "I'm sorry. You've just never..." he paused for a moment. "It's like you're– "

"Different?"

"Yes." He nodded. She came to sit beside him and held his hand. It felt warm and affectionate despite her cutting remarks. "I think we've both been under a spell. Made to live like..."

"Like what?" she asked, noticing that his dark eyes were absorbed in her angelic face.

"I don't know. Like prisoners, I think. I can come and go but I can't leave this island. It's like a prison and *he* has all the keys."

"I think you're right," she said quietly, lowering her head.

"Look at me," he lifted her chin gently with his hand. "You've broken free now. What will you do next?" He felt he had carelessly flung his soul into the air, waiting for her to catch it.

"Stop him," she replied. "He's going to hurt the others."

"What others?"

"There were people stranded here. He told me he brought them here. I didn't see how it was possible but I read his journals last night."

Jet's stomach sank. *The journals.* He had a stack of them under his bed that Derrien had tried to make him read. "Do you know where?"

"He put them in the jungle. I don't know what happened to them."

"You should stay here and I'll go and see if I can find them. Do you know how many there are?"

She shook her head. "I can guess four, maybe five."

"Where is Geraint?"

"I left him at the sand dunes. I showed him the way back to the cottage but... Oh what have I done?" She held her face in her hands and shook her head.

"It's all right. I'll see if I can find him." Grabbing his jacket, he rushed to the door and opened it, turning to look at Thea one last time. She rushed to the door and grabbed the handle. He waited for her to say something or do something, but she stood there, silent.

He could see that whatever she had wanted to do, she had no intention of following it through. She had no will to continue their conversation or run after him, so she stepped back and let him leave, crying as the door closed behind him.

13

B althazar entered the bridge of the Demeter. The auto lights did not come on when he unlocked the doors. *Funny* he thought. He searched around for a light switch. That was when he saw it.

The creature rattled around behind the captain's chair. Its shadow seemed to cover the room depending on its position.

"I walk through the valley of the shadow of death..." Balthazar began to whisper but no matter how much he tried, he could only think of the lyrics of an old rap song and not the much needed psalm. "Computer, lights!"

No response. He could hear the hissing behind the captain's chair. "W-whatever you want, j-just take it," he stuttered, the freezing instinct gripped him by the gut and held him there. "I just want the comms s-system, yeah?" The hissing continued. "Lights!" he commanded. The darkness withstood his newly discovered authoritative tone.

He decided to abandon the mission and head back to his cabin. As he swiped his fob across the lock panel, nothing happened. He ran it past the panel again and again. He tried wiping his fob against his shirt and then swiping. Nothing. He was locked in there with the thing.

"Liana. Lights."

"Balthazar! Are you going to ask nicely?" *Oh thank god,* he thought.

"Liana, please turn the lights on." The creature was drawing closer to him. He could feel its warm breath against his cheek. He clamped his eyes closed and held his breath.

"Balthazar, what are you doing here in the dark?" Liana was sitting in the captain's chair, cross legged and smiling. The bridge was fully lit with all control panels working and flickering. Their reassuring hums and bleeps made him take a deep breath.

"Liana, please plot a course for Atlantis from Oceanus."

"Oh honey," she shook her head, "we can't plot courses for planets that aren't in the database."

"You can't? How does anyone get back then?"

"They have to map it."

"I don't know how to do that."

"Me neither honey. Those are just the rules." She was admiring her pink fingernails.

"Let's send another distress call out then."

"Sure thing." She winked and turned to open the computer. "Oh wait a minute."

"What is it?"

"It's a message!" she said excitedly. "It's for you."

Balthazar leaned over to the computer Liana was sitting at. It was a message from the Atlantis Science Council. For a moment, he could only stare at the message notification. "Open it."

***

B Swaine,

Message received. We are unable to provide assistance. our message was tracked as originating from a system that we have no jurisdiction in.

Your message has been forwarded to the relevant bodies who may be able to issue emergency legislation, but this is unlikely at present. We have also notified New Botswana, The Rimar and Atlantis of the S.S Demeter's status.

End transmission.

***

Balthazar's stomach sank deeper than he thought humanly possible. He didn't breathe for some time. "Is this all of it?" he asked.

"I think so. That was the end of transmission there." she pointed at the red line on the screen.

"They're not coming." he felt his breath shortening and tried to stay calm. He rested a hand on Liana's shoulder.

"What will you do next?"

"Me?" He had forgotten that he was indeed on his own, no matter how helpful Liana was. "I don't know. Can we scan for life signs?"

"Of course."

Within seconds, new data appeared on the screen.

Human: 13

Uncategorised: 2

Liana swiped to reveal a three dimensional computerised blueprint of the planet. "Those red dots are where the humans are." The small planet consisted mostly of ocean with one small land mass. To the north of the island was a cluster of five red dots. To the south of it was one red dot heading north. On the eastern edge of the island was another cluster of six red dots. In the centre, there was one red dot. On the same point of the map was a white dot and another white dot further to the south west of the island. "The white dots are uncategorised. Either the body temperatures are out of regular parameters or the scanners have detected other organic life forms by mistake."

"Other organic life forms? Like, cows for example?" He didn't know why the cow was the first animal that came to mind. "Please tell me it means animals."

Liana turned to look at him gravely. "Animals are usually categorised as animal or 'organic/other,'" she said.

"What?" Balthazar's heart was racing. "You mean?" He couldn't bring himself to say *alien*.

"It's possible," Liana nodded.

"Oh my god." Balthazar felt sick with giddiness. "Ok, do we know if they're dangerous?"

"No way of knowing but the humans on the planet are alive so that's a good sign."

"We're only missing five, maybe seven." he started to count on his fingers. "Captain, co-pilot, Engineer guy, comms guy, me..." he struggled to name anyone else.

"I could pull up the personnel report for you?"

"Excellent. Let's do that."

The list contained eleven names including the crew and the passengers. "What? There are eleven people on the planet." Balthazar was stunned. "Who the hell are the other two?"

"It's not clear," Liana said.

"Do we have any chance of finding out who these guys are?" Balthazar swiped across to return to the blueprint. The same red dots were flashing.

"Not really. I can find shuttles and see who piloted if that helps?"

"Yes please. Scan for shuttles."

Liana retrieved new information to display on the screen. This time, there were four vessels. Three were flashing green and one was blue. "What does blue mean, Liana?"

"It means unserviceable. This is the Io and it appears to be broken down or damaged... and it's in a body of water. Doesn't look good."

"Can we get it back up and running?"

"Maybe. Want me to see if I can fire up the ship's tractor beam? There doesn't seem to be a storm today."

"Yes please, Liana. See if you can get that shuttle back in action." Liana tapped away on the other consoles, swiping screens and pushing buttons. Balthazar, despite his copious reading of the previous twenty four hours, felt so far out of his depth that he happily watched Liana work. He sat in the captain's chair, watching the life signs on the overhead screen with bated breath.

The two white dots stirred deep feelings of fear mixed with fascination. He wondered if this was an opportunity to seize or a catastrophe to avoid. He wished he wasn't in charge any more.

14

— . —

Beneath the small sandstone cottage at the edge of the lake, the first expeditioners had built an underground laboratory. It was in this laboratory that Shona and Paul Lennox worked into the early hours every night. After Paul had died, Shona continued the work alone while their child slept. It was in this laboratory where Derrien had continued the work— powerless to do otherwise.

Having found himself with the journals in his hands, he had learned of Shona's true intentions and questioned the things she had done in the name of science. He had found himself disappointed by her self-ishness and horrified by her actions. However, this knowledge didn't stop him from following in her footsteps with due diligence.

From the endless journal archives he found, he had learned that she had returned to the planet after the Interplanetary Science Council had declared the planet and its system a dead zone. Shona Lennox had wanted to return to Oceanus so badly that she revisited with her husband and son, losing the former soon after. What made Derrien feel worst of all was the realisation that dozens had done it before her. He had read journal entries from terraformers and biologists dating back to 2205.

He had spent hours poring over pages and pages of data and felt all the worse for it. Derrien had abhorred Shona's decisions when he had learned of them but found himself unable to do anything differently.

All night he had worked; sleep did not come to him easily. No amount of chamomile tea, cool temperatures or darkness could help him drift off into the land of nod, so he worked. He worked until he drove himself mad with hallucinations.

Shona visited every now and then, reminding him that he needed to get off the planet as soon as possible. She would sometimes frighten him with her sudden appearance. He never really knew how long she'd been there, watching him.

The more he ignored her, the more cadaverous she became until she rotted away into nothingness.

"All right, fine. We can talk," he said, addressing the air.

Shona reappeared, smiling. She looked healthy and alive. No longer did her face bring horror. She was once more wearing her white lab coat. "You have to cut your ties with R.E.L," she said gently, sitting down in the chair beside him.

Derrien folded his arms. "But it makes me so powerful. Man shouldn't have such powers and yet, here I am." He gave her a dark smile.

"I know, Derrien. I thought it was amazing too but..." she looked to the door behind them and spoke in a quieter voice, "it's going to kill you all." For the first time in his life, he saw genuine fear in Shona's eyes.

"You thought that once."

"But I was right, wasn't I? I wasn't right about how I handled it but it's too much power for us. We can't contain it." She looked back at the door again, "and we certainly can't use it."

"It could be the psionic awakening we've always needed," he pleaded. She remained fearful. Her eyes were wide and flitting from him to the back door.

"But it's much more likely that it spells the end for mankind."

"You're just being conservative."

"Derrien, deny me all you want but you know deep down that I'm right. If I was wrong, why is R.E.L still in a tank at the back of this room?"

He paused for a moment, glancing up at the door she was referring to. "Because you put it there," he said quietly, looking down at the red mark on his forearm.

"Because it's *dangerous*, Derrien." She looked at him earnestly. "It showed me the end of my life. It showed me the end of all life as we know it. It even showed me—"

"I know. But they didn't come, did they?"

"No." She cast her eyes down at her lap. "But if that doesn't tell you that it causes harm, I don't know what will." She looked at the door again. "It was able to cheat me out of everything I loved. Everything I cared about. I became a monster. I cared about nothing but the power this thing had and look what happened. God, I was *so certain* that I knew what I was doing. You are certain that you know what you're doing but I can tell you now, Derrien– you're going to die."

"They thought androids were declaring war on the human race. They were wrong about that..."

"They were not. Synthetics have been outlawed for a hundred and fifty years and *you know* why. This thing is far worse than synthetics."

"Oh Shona. Just think of the potential," he said. *'The potential'*. He thought of all *'the potential'* that had come before. He struggled to think of any *'potential'* that had truly helped mankind in his living memory. In the face of former catastrophes, Derrien still believed that this time was different. This time, *he* was right– or so he thought. Shona did not agree.

"Derrien," she snapped, "you are going down a path that is running out of escape routes. Many a fool before Derrien Victor Smith thought they could harness powers that were greater than they were and do you know what happened? They overestimated themselves. Humanity had a close brush with extinction. Man is an insignificant speck of stardust compared with the rest of the universe." She placed her hand on his. "Some things are greater than we are. That's a fact of life." She stood up and folded her arms. "I learned that the hard way."

Derrien thought of the accident and the night he discovered what Shona had done. A cold chill trickled down his back. "Don't make the same mistakes that I did. I know the lure is so strong," she said, placing a hand on his shoulder. "It washed over me and for the first time in my life, my work was going somewhere. I had discovered alien life and it was giving me the power to..." she held her hand to her mouth and shook her head. "The power is so strong. So very strong but you cannot let it take you. We are not ready for this kind of power. Get off this bloody planet and save my son. I wasn't capable, Derrien. I still believe that you are."

"It's too late, Shona." Derrien turned his back to her. "They're all going to die."

"No!" She spun him around in the chair to face her wrath. "You will not condemn them to death."

He fell to the floor in blinding pain. The zigzag streaks of silver blinded him as he scrunched his eyes closed and held his head. "Stop it, please," he begged. Shona stood over him, her face solemn. He writhed and convulsed as she watched him roll around the floor, vomiting until he was still.

15

— • —

Thea lay on the bed listening to the birds singing in the trees outside the woodcutter's hut. Bright, blinding sunshine peered in through the partially open window. The lake, as always, lay veiled by the morning mist that dampened the air around it. She had drifted between sleeping and waking for hours through the night, overwhelmed with the weight of her own thoughts. Some thoughts were welcomed. Others, not so much.

The darkness of the night terrified her at times as though she were a child again. She would trick herself into following shadows around the room. Other times, she would wake up and not know where she was. She had been alone for the entire time. Alone with nothing but new and demanding contemplations for company. Alone, these persisted and grew into troubling dreams. Many faces appeared before her including a face that she could barely remember. It was a face that looked like hers but she couldn't touch it. It was too far away.

In her most vivid dream, she floated beneath the lake, looking up at waves of liquid silver and a giant, burning ball of light that she couldn't reach. Bubbles escaped from her tight lips slowly but they were running out. Her hair floated around her face, clouding her vision. Nothing but the doom of cold, weightless darkness lay beneath her. She gently circled her arms and kicked her bare legs to rise upwards, increasing the intensity. The surface seemed to roll away from her, sweeping from her fingertips as she reached out. She kicked harder, the tension in her muscles throwing her upwards and upwards until finally, she gasped that intoxicating pull of oxygen from the surface and felt the cold grip of air on her bare, wet shoulders. She woke from that dream gasping, sweating and coughing. It felt too real.

In her state of exhaustion, she would drift off again. At times– in other dreams– she would find herself lost on a raft at sea, trying to navigate the black waters of Oceanus in the cold, bleak, ominous night. The sky, merciless in its blanketed clouds, withheld the stars from her in the darkness. Some time would pass as she sat upright on the raft. It was now morning. She would make out the outline of a little girl on the shore, collecting things and placing them in a bag or basket. Thea would call for help as the raft drifted slightly closer on the waves. The child could not hear her. Thea waved and called again. Her voice would not carry across the troubled waters. The little girl walked away.

She woke up trembling, and felt as though she had been brought back from the brink of drowning to death again and again.

Thea wondered if she had ever dreamed before last night.

In the moments that held her between waking and sleeping, her mind led her to memories of Jet. She had seen Jet's face a thousand times, always feeling that it wasn't enough. When he had returned to her, four years before, she could barely remember him. This hurt him, as had most of the things she had done or said but he continued to live nearby on the other side of the loch. He had remained an unconditional friend to her when she had none. It was no secret that he despised her father and this realisation baffled her; she had never asked why. Thea accepted it with a child-like innocence, as she had done with everything then.

Her final dream that night had disturbed her most of all. She saw Jet fade away with old age, alone. He sat on the dock, struggling to look up or speak to her. He was so old, so worn and frail as she rowed away from him to the centre of the loch.

He had not noticed the flower crown on her head, assembled with laurels and roses from her own garden. He had not even looked in her direction. She drifted away from him. Unable to breathe, she lay down and silently died in the boat. She could see that Jet hadn't noticed that she had left his side. She watched her own death from the edge of the lake. Her perfectly formed, youthful corpse lay to rest on a bed of flowers.

The row boat, after some time, eventually found its way back to shore where Jet was grief-stricken. As the old, withered man looked down upon her lifeless face, he returned to his youth instantaneously. He could not see her watching him from the other side of the lake. She saw that she was dead to him and he was all the better for it. That particular dream had left her feeling hollow when she woke.

That morning, when she decided to give up on her fight for sleep, she had stretched, grazing the top of Jet's pillow with her fingertips. She flinched for a second, as though she had touched it without permission. Intrigued by her own feeling of hesitation, she moved closer to the pillow and inhaled. It smelled of him. His scent delighted her. She held the pillow close to her and reflected on the events of the night before; it left her with a heavy sadness. She treated the symptom with happier thoughts and so the cycle continued from the moment she had first given herself time to think.

Thought is free, she reflected and smiled. She had read and reread his entire collection of books, she liked his smell and enjoyed being in his cabin. Jet Lennox was her favourite person in the entire world. She hated herself for the things she had said the previous night. On reflection, she hadn't meant any of it. Her eye spied *Wuthering Heights* on his bookshelf. "I am as cruel as Katherine," she said to herself and buried her face in the pillow. She thought of all the literary heroines in his books and decided that she did not want to be a Katherine, an Estella or a Delilah. She wanted to prioritise love and give love freely and stubbornly like Jane. She wanted to be an honest and devoted Miranda. She realised that she *could* be anyone she wanted to be. When she thought of him, the desire to see him and the despondency from his absence scared her.

The familiar thrill she felt when she had kissed him returned to her at the very thought of him. It had taken her by surprise at first and forced her to suppress it. She had lied to him and to herself; the thought of never being able to see him again and tell him caused fresh tears to well up in her already tired and red-rimmed eyes. She sobbed into the pillow. The compulsion to cry was uncontrollable. The logical explanation was nowhere to be seen.

Some time later, Thea reluctantly rose from the bed and lit the stove, heating up some water for tea. While she waited, she splashed her face with cold water, wetting some of her hair as she did so.

As she sat back down on the bed and sipped the tea, she wondered if Jet had been able to find Geraint and the other people. She felt sick, realising that she feared for his safety. Of course, she was concerned for Geraint and the others but she wished to see Jet again above all. She thought of little else. Her mind was growing tired from all the thinking; some muscles in her mind had never been flexed before. She sipped her tea.

As all thoughts did, another led to thoughts of her father. She had read his notes from the previous two days. He had even told her what he had done but she could only hear. Listening had been beyond her at that time.

The timeline of events unravelled before her eyes, starting with the moment she saw Geraint's shuttle sinking into the lake in the storm her father had summoned.

She was starkly reminded of his limp, drowning body and his pale lips as he lay unconscious in the bed. She hadn't understood what it all meant. She hadn't understood why her father was so solemn. She hadn't understood life and death.

She looked over at the photograph of Shona Lennox. A memory came flooding back to the forefront of her mind: death.

Distracted, she dropped the cup, scalding her hand as she vainly attempted to catch it in mid air. The burn intensified as she watched it with amazement. The chamomile and honey liquid dripped away onto her skirt, cooling her palm with the breath of the chilled morning air. She could not recall the last time that she had been injured, if ever. The sting caused her hand to twitch but she could not bring herself to move. It was as though she had never seen her own hand before. It was white, delicate and as beautiful as she had ever hoped to have for a hand. She raised the other one to admire them together. "*What lovely things hands are.*" she said. She looked down at her feet, too. She loved them as well. They were positioned next to the small cup that she had dropped onto the bare wood floor. She knelt down to pick it up and retrieved a towel for the spilled tea.

While she was dabbing the spill with the towel, she saw that some had spilled on to a stack of journals under the bed. Rather than ignore them and go about her business, she felt the urge to drag them out onto the bed and read them intently. The journal at the bottom of the stack was dated 2298. The journal at the top was dated 2311. She recognised her father's handwriting. A paralysing chill shot up her spine. She began to read.

16

— · —

B y midday, Jet had searched the empty cottage, scoured the beach and the brushlands around it and hadn't found even a hint of Geraint's existence. If Derrien was around, Jet had not noticed. The lake and the cottage were deserted. In a sense, he was glad that he hadn't bumped into Derrien since the incident with the axe. The little row boat on the dock rocked gently. The birds and rabbits on the sand dunes went about their business. Jet was the only one who seemed restless.

Part of him didn't want to find Geraint. Part of him didn't care about anyone. The other part wanted to do the right thing. That part, he knew, would do anything if Thea had asked it of him.

He marched across the island under the brooding grey clouds and bristling winds. The grass on the sand dunes whispered to him as he passed to look across the beach one more time in case he had missed footprints. He found no trace.

In his exasperation, he decided that he would have to make his way to the jungle and hope to find Geraint there. He tried not to think too much of the kiss Thea had told him of. *Had Thea enjoyed that?* He wondered with a sneer, thinking of the time she kissed him and immediately declared that she felt nothing as a result. The gut punch was unavoidable. He imagined Geraint, handsome in his finery, kissing Thea in her garden. It infuriated him. He marched on, slashing bamboo and ferns out of his path with his machete.

After some time of forcing his way through the brush like a juggernaut, Jet found a trail. Someone else had walked there ahead of him. It circled around a spot where he supposed the same someone was now resting, but Jet – more than accustomed to his surroundings– knew better than to jump in before assessing the danger.

It had not taken him long for him to find Geraint. He was sat on a fallen tree, smacking himself to neutralise the mosquitos. He seemed tired.

Jet had lingered, hidden in the trees at first, throwing small rocks to see what Geraint would do. As he expected, Geraint was nervous and without a weapon. He eventually took pity on him and revealed himself.

For a moment, the two young men regarded each other with a stern suspicion.

Realising that the savage before him may not be accustomed to manners, Geraint held out a hand with no expectation. "You must be Jet," he said to the tall, olive-skinned stranger. Jet wore clothing similar to Derrien- an open-necked linen peasant shirt and light trousers. Unlike Derrien, he was clean with slicked black hair with a wanton curl hanging over his forehead. He carried a bundle of rope and canvas on his back. On his belt, he carried some tools. Geraint, in contrast, had nothing with him and was grateful for Jet's arrival as he couldn't build a fire and was hopelessly lost. That was not what he told Jet, though. "I was just thinking of making camp here," he said with feigned assurance. Jet, as predicted, did not take his hand. He returned it to his side sheepishly and put his hands in his pockets. There was no friendliness to be found on Jet's sultry face. "It was time to take a rest," Geraint began, "it's not that hard to get around jungles. They're all much of a muchness, aren't they? Once you've seen one, you've seen them all."

Jet thought back to the circular trail he had followed to get to Geraint and said nothing.

"I might know where they are," Jet said. "Follow me." He turned on his heel and walked away.

Geraint did as he was told and accompanied Jet into the dense thicket of ferns and trees, taking care to step in Jet's footprints. He occasionally shot a glance back over his shoulder. It had not been long after they set off walking that Geraint started to feel as though he was being followed. He shook it off at first but the rustling behind him grew louder, begging for his attention. In the warmth of the jungle air, Geraint was chilled to the bone. He felt underdressed and shivered uncontrollably. His teeth began to chatter as the muscles in his jaw convulsed, trying desperately to warm him up. When Geraint stopped, the noise stopped. The cool trickles of fear down his back persisted, although he had been brave enough to check himself; He wanted to make sure nothing was trailing behind him but he could not steady himself. There was something there.

"Jet," Geraint whispered.

"Yeah?" Jet, as though he had been interrupted during an important meeting, turned around to look at him.

"There's something behind us."

Jet peered into the thick ferns behind them. Saying nothing, he shrugged and shook his head. Geraint, embarrassed, nodded and they continued in silence all but for some crunching of leaves and snapping of twigs underfoot. Geraint was thirsty, tired and sick of Oceanus. He wanted to go home. Home was where he could find his own bed, sleep where he was welcome, play with his dog, read his books and do whatever he wanted. Oceanus struck him with the reality of his absolute helplessness. He hated it. There were no comforts to be found on the entire planet. He felt that it was barren and the people were cold to him. It was too quiet for his liking, too moody and there was something considerably ominous and unwelcoming about it. He would be glad to put it behind him, he thought.

He studied Jet for a while, listening to see if he even breathed, he was so quiet. Jet Lennox strode through the foliage as though it were nothing, while Geraint wrestled with vines and palm leaves slapping him in the face. The insects didn't seem to bother Jet, either. Geraint, irritated by his own perspiration, was flummoxed by how his guide didn't seem to even glisten in the humidity of the jungle.

For the next few yards, Geraint still felt something closing in on him. It was walking within his shadow, breathing heavily. He resolved to walk faster, keeping up with Jet's long-legged pace. The thing behind him sped up, too.

Geraint tried to tell Jet to stop and turn around but it was no use. He felt as though his throat was closing over. He focused on Jet's long, black hair in front of him that melted into the smothering darkness that comes with losing consciousness.

It was breathing down his neck by the time they reached the pit.

"Jet" Geraint gargled, trying to remove the fingers that were clenched around his neck. "Jet!" he cried louder. Jet turned around and looked right at him with an expression of impatience that soon turned to surprise.

"What is it?" He was taken aback with horror as Geraint lost colour.

Geraint crumpled to the ground, choking and gasping for air. A vine was wrapped around his neck. Jet grabbed his pocket knife and cut it. Geraint passed out. "Hey," Jet gave him a gentle slap on the face. "Hey, you can't do that here." Jet shook him without success. "You can't do this here," he said earnestly. "Stay awake." It was starting to rain.

When Geraint didn't stir, Jet sighed in annoyance and lifted him over his shoulder, placing him back down when he reached the nearest sheltering tree. When Geraint finally opened his eyes and groaned, he looked into Jet's face with a sharp, noticeable fear in his eyes. "You'll think I'm mad but..." Geraint coughed severely, holding his neck. "That wasn't me." He pointed to the red mark on his neck. "I didn't do that."

"I didn't see anything," Jet said. He looked around at the canopy above him, listening for sounds that did not belong. "But I believe you," he said quietly, looking away.

When Geraint was able to stand again, they approached the pit with caution. It was a sheer drop and the rain was splashing down from the canopy. "The mud will soften and start falling in. We don't have much time," Jet said, looking up at the sky, "call for them."

"Dad?" Geraint called down with his hands cupped. He couldn't see anything in the opaqueness of the hole, nor could he lean in any further. "Dad!"

"Geraint?" Owen called. "We're down here, son!"

"All of you?"

"All of us!"

"How many?"

"Five, but Anthony is unconscious."

The two young men looked at each other. "We'll build a sling," Jet said calmly. "Although there isn't enough time to do it right now. The rain is getting heavier. Tell him someone will need to stay with him." Jet laid the rope out.

"Dad, we can't get Anthony right now. Someone needs to stay with him." Geraint called into the pit. It seemed endless but he didn't dare lean in further. Jet was poised like a cat waiting to catch him.

"Ok, hang on," said Owen.

Faint murmuring could be heard for a couple of minutes as Geraint and Jet waited anxiously, trying not to sink into the mud. "Three of us to come up," Owen said.

Jet started tying a rope to the nearest tree. "Grab this," he said, throwing the end of it to Geraint. "Throw it down there. They're going to have to pull themselves up."

Jet had secured his and Geraint's waists with a safety line. "Just in case," he said with the same lack of expression he gave to everything that afternoon. Geraint swallowed and nodded.

Much to Geraint's surprise, lifting his father, Seb and Ade wasn't as hard as he had worried it would be. Jet seemed to be able to pull on the rope with inhuman strength, securing his heels without slipping into the pit. The rain was falling heavily by the time Ade was rescued. He clambered on to the earth and gripped the rope for dear life, mud and rain obscuring his vision. "I hate heights," he wheezed. Jet scooped him up from his underarms and dragged him away from the pit to the tree he was secured to.

Owen embraced his son firmly. They stayed locked together for a minute or so.

"Thank you," Seb said, holding out a hand to Jet. Jet hesitantly shook it. "I'm Seb."

"I'm Jet."

Seb regarded the young man for a moment. "You live here?" He eyed him from head to toe. He was dressed in handmade clothing. Seb thought it was remarkable but tried not to stare. "It was hard to leave Trin, our science officer," he said. "She volunteered to stay with Anthony but I'd rather she wasn't stuck there for long."

"We just have to wait for this rain to pass and I'll get them out, otherwise we could collapse the pit on them," Jet assured him.

When Owen had finally let go of his son, he also shook Jet's hand. "Thank you." He patted him on the back. "I'm Owen. Thank you for helping Geraint."

Jet looked over at the exhausted Geraint. "Geraint was already on his way here. If anything, he helped me." He looked away to study the downpour.

Owen beamed at his son who was untying the safety line from his waist. He cast a glance at Ade who was cleaning himself up and to Seb who was rearranging their bags.

"What about Trin and Anthony?"

"We need to build a sling for him but we can't do it right now," Jet said loudly through the driving rain. "We have to make camp and come back when it's dry."

"I've left Trin with the sedatives, just in case," Ade said.

Jet looked to Owen, who nodded and said, "Anthony isn't well. He is having hallucinations."

Jet collected the rope and proceeded with wrapping it across his arm. "We'll make camp nearby but they can use this." He gave Owen some canvas and rope.

"Trin!" Owen called into the darkness.

"Yes, I'm here," she said.

"Trin, I'm going to throw some canvas down and some wood. We will come back for you when it's safe."

"Ok. Chuck it!" she shouted. Owen let the bundle drop down the pit. "Received!" she called up from the black hole.

The men made camp twenty yards from the pit where the trees were dense and provided a natural umbrella for the rain. Jet, without entertaining any discussion, set to work on the fire while the others built their tents. Owen and Geraint watched him work as they built their tent a few yards away.

"Where did he come from?" Owen whispered to Geraint.

"He lives here," his son said quietly.

"Does he? By himself?" Owen asked, looking at Jet's face glowing in the newly lit flames.

"No." Geraint shook his head. "There are others here. A guy called Derrien…" he was distracted for a moment thinking about how bizarre his experience had been, "and his daughter."

Owen stiffened. *Derrien*. He had not heard the name in years. "Derrien?" he asked. "Unusual name."

"Yeah, I thought that, too. He was stranded here a long time ago."

Geraint looked at his father and observed his greying, wan face. "Geraint." A sickening twist of guilt squeezed Owen's stomach. He felt heavy. "I think I know Derrien. Is he…Derrien Victor Smith?"

"Yes. That's him!"

Owen's legs seemed to fail him. Geraint caught him as he stumbled, generating some concerned looks from the others. "Son," Owen said gravely. "There's something I need to tell you but you mustn't say a word."

17

Balthazar stared at the blinking lights on the screen. *Uncategorised.* He still wasn't sure what to do about it. Even as a simpleton– as he often referred to himself– he knew that the protocol was to run and get out of there as soon as possible but he couldn't bring himself to do it. Never before in his life had he been faced with tough decisions. "This will be good for you," his father had said when he informed his parents of his new career. "It will be the making of you."

Balthazar did not want to be made today but he had to.

He had resolved to bring the shuttles back and everyone on them. As it stood, he was on his own, in space, with nothing but a hallucination for assistance.

"We can bring them all back, clean 'em up and send them back down?" Liana suggested. She looked up at him, blinking in a way that was beginning to annoy him.

"What if something goes wrong though?" He sensed his own impatience in his voice. He wanted to say, "I'm sorry," but now that the fear of the uncategorised throbbed in his stomach, he couldn't spare a thought for niceties. *Come on Balthazar,* he thought.

"What if it does go wrong? You've always done things the wrong way because you're so fucking stupid," a voice whispered from the shadows of the bridge.

"Stop it," Balthazar said.

Liana spun around in her chair. "What?"

"Not you."

"They're all going to die down there and it's your fault. You're an idiot who can barely count to ten and you know it."

Balthazar coughed nervously and turned away from Liana. He stared into the shadows in the corner of the room. It waited for him, smiling in the dark. His eyes met with his tormentor.

"Bugger off," he said.

It hissed in the black recesses, laughing at him.

"Bugger. Off," he said again firmly.

It was still laughing at him. "I'm not afraid of you any more. You know that. You can stay if you want but this is the last time I notice, mate." He turned his back to the shadow.

"What's going on?"

"Liana, listen. I know you're a computer system and you appearing as this..." he held out his hands and circled them, "person... it's just a way of me processing things I can't really understand. You're hot and interesting and you hold my attention more than a guidebook could but this is the last thing we do together." He smiled. "It's been a pleasure, but I don't need help any more."

"Are you sure?" she asked.

He nodded, acknowledging the reality of his situation. He looked at his aide and thought about all of the imaginary friends who had sat with him in the classrooms over the years. The imaginary friends that had rubbed his back when he cried on the school steps. The friends who, when he was nine, helped him to make sense of his homework when he had the reading age of a four-year-old. His parents, on several occasions, had thrust their only son at the feet of various specialists and counsellors. "Selective mute," their notes would say. The little boy would shut down, hiding within himself and unable to hear any calls–no matter how supportive, from his parents. In his head he would have already ran away to be with his friends, off on an adventure. They understood everything and could explain it to him in a way that was manageable. They took the difficult things away.

As he looked at Liana, he smiled and prepared himself to say goodbye to his final imaginary friend. "It's about time I sorted things out myself from now on," he said with a sigh. "We'll go through the shuttle reactivation and I'll take it from there." He pulled at his lapels. "You just show me all the buttons, yeah?" He turned to look at the shadow creature. It was gone.

Liana, seeming satisfied, smiled and turned back to the console. "We could just reactivate them from here. Do you want me to try that? The Io is a write off but the others should work."

"Please, Liana."

He watched Liana as she tapped away on the keys, bringing countless maps, coordinates and blueprints onto the screen. "Hmm, I might need to drag them out," she frowned. He studied the symbols and notifications as they appeared, following the lines of the blueprints.

"What about the uncategorised? Will they be able to get on the shuttles?" Balthazar was nervous but instead of doing nothing as was the usual response, he had already imagined an unauthorised boarding scenario including three possible outcomes. Although none were successful, he had been delighted to have worked it out by himself. He knew that he wouldn't be able to stop it as a one man defence and was prepared to think of something else as he observed Liana zooming in on each shuttle.

"The uncategorised are nowhere near the shuttles. I really wouldn't worry. It could be an anomaly. I'm sure if they're supposed to be human, one of the survivors will be able to tell us."

"Ok." That reassured him. "Let's try and bring the shuttles– oh, wait!" He thought for a moment. "What if we can't get them back down there? It's better to keep them where they're useful."

Liana zoomed in on a shuttle that had three red dots inside it and was positioned on the east of the island. "If this one is manned, do you think it should come up?"

"Yes. Is it stuck, though?"

"Maybe. We could just try contacting them on the emergency channel?"

"Let's do that."

Liana tapped away again on the console. "The scanner shows this one is stuck in a rock face but there are five humans on board... and they're alive."

Well of course they're alive, the screen says so, he thought. "Good," was his final, filtered response. Balthazar pulled the receiver out of its cap and opened a channel, "S.S Demeter to Europa, do you read me?"

The line buzzed for a while with some minor scraping sounds. "This is the S.S Demeter to Europa." He held his breath for a moment, thinking of the men on the shuttle. They were alive according to the scanners but in what state? "Can I leave this on a loop?" he asked Liana quietly.

She nodded. "Sure." She tapped a button with one perfectly man-icured finger like a twentieth century air hostess flipping the smoking light back on. "It's on loop now."

"Can we do the same for Callisto?" He eyed the location of the other two shuttles on the map. They had no people on board. He noticed that there was a fourth, larger vessel on the island, too." He pointed to it.

"Still no information on that one?"

"It says classified. It won't tell me."

"Classified? But this is a rescue mission."

"I've tried, honey, but it won't let me in. I don't have the security codes. I'm just a computer, remember?" She flashed her lovely Hollywood smile, the kind he'd seen in the vintage cinemas his mother took him to as a child. She was delightful and he loved her, but she wasn't real.

She was indeed, just a computer. He could bring anyone or anything to life thanks to years of self-isolation. He thought about whether or not that was a sort of superpower– having a powerful imagination. He was able to fantasise and live the difficulties out, solving them in real time. Liana had been vital for helping him come up with a solution but she was happy to handover to Balthazar, as all good friends were.

"Balthazar Swaine. Cabin Steward... and more," he said to himself. He was going to rescue the crew and he was going to do it now. *Check this out, Dad,* he thought. He wished Hamza Swaine was there to see him confidently communicating with the stranded vessels. Given his track record, he did wonder for a moment if anyone would believe him this time. "Ok, let's just keep what I said on loop and maybe someone will answer when the weather changes. Is that how things work down there? Interference?"

"Well, there was an ion storm when they landed down there. It could have jammed some signals or damaged sensors. I don't know what state the shuttles will be in today but it's likely that there is some hardware damage. Possibly even from emergency landing. Shuttles on envoy ships aren't really as robust as the other kinds you find. They're just A to B ships."

"Ok, thanks. Is it ready to go now?"

"Yes. I've set it up to broadcast across all three communication systems."

"Ok." Balthazar took a deep breath. "This is Balthazar Swain of the S.S Demeter. Please respond."

Balthazar had decided to spend the rest of the day on the bridge in the hope that one shuttle would respond. The Europa was the only one with life signs showing. He pinned all of his hopes on her and dozed in the captain's chair.

Several hours had passed when, half asleep, he thought he heard another voice speaking to him. It was not Liana's.

"This is Captain Walner piloting the Europa," came a man's voice through the channel accompanied by crackling and humming. "Who am I speaking to?"

Balthazar leapt out of the chair onto the floor. He clambered back up and clumsily grabbed the receiver. His throat tightened. *Thank God* he thought. "Captain Walner. This is Cabin Steward Balthazar Swaine. How many men do you have with you?"

"Four, Mr Swaine." There was a pause. "We have been wedged in a cave for two days."

"Captain, I would like to propose that we pull you out with the tractor beam."

There was another pause.

"You will have to redistribute power from the main engine for this, Mr Swaine."

"I am willing to do that, sir."

"Ok. The tide seems to be coming in. If I were you, I would wait until it has gone back out before attempting to pull us out." There was a momentary pause, followed by more crackling. "It's going to be about eight hours from now."

18

—·—

"Wake up, my love," called a woman's voice from downstairs.

Anthony was still sleeping but he smiled as though his mother was in the room. It was early morning. He could hear the robin and the blackbird competing for the limelight with their songs outside his window. The slits in the blinds warmed his face with thin beams of gentle sunshine. The cool morning breeze of a summer's day sighed into his ears as he rolled over. He did not remember dreaming that night.

He opened his eyes, rubbed the sleep away, yawned and stretched. Looking around in surprise, he saw that he was in his old bed, in his old house and judging by his hands and feet, he was eight or nine again. He looked across to the bed on the left. The duvet was scrunched into a creased snail origami with the pillow hanging off the edge. He smiled. His brother was already up.

The landing was silent. Footlights slowly turned on and off as he passed each one to get to the top of the stairs. Across from him, on the front wall of the house, there was a floor to ceiling window showing him the sapphire sea and the marina. The little white boats bobbed in the morning mist. The sun was rising quickly, reaching up the stairs with warm, precise sunbeams.

He carefully held the polished wood handrail and softly glided down the stairs, gingerly laying a bare foot on each carpeted step, feeling the fibres bristle against his skin. They creaked in the exact same places as he remembered. He grabbed both rails for the last three steps and swung his body over them, landing with a solid thump on the living room's hard floor, as he had always done.

The mechanical clock ticked quietly on the mantelpiece. It was an antique from twentieth century Earth that had been left to his mother by her mother, and her mother before that. It was eight o'clock in the morning, judging by the little ding of the clock's bell.

He wandered through the living room, running a hand across the back of the sofa. It was red, just as he had remembered. He had been happiest in this home.

While he was standing still, a little tinkle of another bell accompanied by a meow startled him. Soft fur brushed against the back of his legs as his cat, Jimbo, made a figure of eight around his ankles. "You can't call a cat Jimbo," his father had protested at first. However, the little ginger kitten thrilled his son and had, by extension, worked its magic on him until he eventually accepted it. "Jimbo," he would mutter, shaking his head in dismay as he laid the cat food down for his son's favourite pet. Anthony knelt down and stroked his ginger tabby. Jimbo purred and closed his green eyes, letting Anthony scratch his white chin. Anthony had always loved Jimbo's white socks in particular. He held one of Jimbo's paws and rubbed a thumb against his cat's pink toes. Jimbo, having had enough of the love and attention, rolled around for a moment and skipped back upstairs as though he had seen a mouse running up them.

At the back of the house, Anthony's mother had laid out the breakfast table with eggs and toast. The tablecloth today was an old fashioned red gingham print with daisies. He had always preferred that one to the others. The chairs were wooden and painted white to match the cupboards. His mother had a habit of painting anything if it stood still for long enough.

Anthony hungrily grabbed some toast and chopped it up into soldiers. He picked up a teaspoon and smashed his way through the top of the egg. He pulled the lid off. Waiting for him inside was the runny, golden yolk. He dipped the soldiers in one by one and devoured them as yolk spilled along the edges of the broken shell. He caught the thick drips with his fingers and licked them off, feeling as though he hadn't eaten in days.

"Steady on," laughed his mother. She was returning from the garden with an empty laundry basket in her arms. Bed sheets and towels were already outside on the washing line, billowing in the breeze like sails on the tall ships of Neverland. She put the basket down in the next room and came to join him at the table, pouring herself some orange juice from the pitcher. He thought that she was the most lovely woman he had ever known and he loved her unconditionally.

He hadn't noticed his seven-year-old brother sitting directly across from him. He was much smaller than Anthony, with a mop of blonde hair and a noticeable cluster of summer freckles across his nose. His dippy egg had also been emptied– every last morsel of white flesh gone. He was drawing a picture now, immersed in his work.

"What's that, darling?" his mother asked, sipping some juice.

"Robot people," the boy muttered, popping a crayon back into the cup.

"Robot people?"

"Yeah. They look just like us… but they're not real." He handed the piece of paper to his mother, who looked at it with sincere interest. "They just do the work and you can switch them off. I thought you would like one to help around the house." He looked up at her and she ruffled his hair.

"Oh darling. That's so sweet of you," she said, holding the drawing in her hands. For the first time, Anthony had observed a flicker of something cross his mother's face. Was it fear? Annalise Victor had never– in her life–feared anything as far as Anthony could see. Although he was a boy again, he watched her with an adult's eyes. Now, she seemed smaller, quieter and distracted.

"Don't encourage him, Annalise," his father said sternly. They looked up to see that he was leaning against the kitchen doorway, finishing his cup of coffee and wearing his uniform. He was ready for work.

Roy Smith was dark like Anthony. His brow was heavy and in a permanent state of pensiveness. He wore his usual boiler suit and carried a tool bag with him to work. Anthony couldn't recall how often his father was at home. For most of their lives, their father had worked as an engineer on various spacecraft. They later learned as teenagers that it had been their mother's decision to keep the family at home on Atlantis rather than on the space stations.

"It's just a picture, Roy," she said quietly over her shoulder. He sighed and picked up his bag.

"I'll see you all tonight."

They listened for the closing of the front door. It clicked shut and their father was gone.

"He should be mad at Anthony," the younger boy whispered.

"Why's that, sweetheart?" his mother asked.

"Anthony's a murderer."

"What?"

Anthony, on hearing his name, froze. He stared at the younger boy with wide eyes. The hot rush of shame reached up through his core and grabbed him by the throat, making it incredibly hard to swallow his saliva. He felt as though he couldn't breathe.

"Anthony, Mummy." The boy pointed directly at Anthony. "He murdered me."

The boy's face began to melt away from his skull, his eyes dripping into the egg shell and filling it back up. Their mother, knocking her chair over as she did so, rose from the table and started screaming. "He murdered me, mummy." The skull rolled on to the table and towards Anthony at speed. "Anthony is a murderer." It kept talking and chattering, its small jaws opening and closing. "Murderer."

***

Trin had built a makeshift tent with some wood, waxed canvas and rope she'd been given by the young man who had rescued the others. Unable to lift Anthony with the materials they had, they left her with what would have been his stretcher. The rain had fallen hard that morning, causing the edges of the pit to slide downwards, splatting cold, thin mud up her bare legs.

Geraint and his companion had promised to return when the mud stopped pouring in. She had no other option but to trust them. The rope that had been used to help the others climb up still hung there. She stared at it from the cover of the tent. The rain trickled through to the pit, gently pattering the surface of the canvas. She could not tell what time of day it was now.

Anthony was still unconscious with his head resting on Owen's jacket. Trin hugged her knees and thought about her companions and what would become of them. As far as she knew, there were five of them plus the stranger. She thought perhaps there would be more people up there. Perhaps the stranger had found the captain and the bridge crew, if they were there at all. Perhaps the Demeter had left. She felt that she would never know.

Anthony intermittently stirred, sighing and muttering. She would jump out of her skin each time as his dreams ripped through her silence. He was not awake, but at least she wasn't alone, she thought.

His nightmares frightened her; her powerlessness frightened her. Not knowing what else to do with the time, she held his hand.

After what seemed like a small eternity for Trin, Anthony jolted awake with a gasp. Their eyes met. He then looked around at the canvas, struggling to form words.

"Hey, shh, it's all right." Trin was blotting his forehead with a cold compress and handed him her flask. "Drink this," she said.

The cooling drips from the neck of the flask and gushes of water flowing down his throat were welcomed by his dry lips. With restraint, he stopped himself from taking all of it and gave the flask back to her. His hands were shaking.

"Where is everyone?"

"Up top. They're coming back for us, don't worry."

"Where did they go?"

"They were rescued, would you believe?"

"Rescued?"

"Yes. At least, I think so. That's what it seemed like. It was Geraint, I think. He had a rope but I said I'd wait with you until they brought a better sling. We'd never have left you here unconscious."

"Geraint?"Anthony half smirked. "As in, Owen's Geraint?"

Trin smiled. "Obviously not *just* Geraint." She looked up again at the fading daylight. "He had help."

"Christ, there *are* people around after all?"

"Yes. I didn't catch his name, or see him actually. Geraint wasn't alone though."

Anthony pushed his arms behind his back and tried to sit up. They trembled under his weight. He groaned with exhaustion. "Best not to do that," Trin said. "They had to tranquilise you."

He winced. "That bad, was it?"

"You were..." she thought for a moment. "It was bad. They all had to pin you down." She shook her head. "It was awful, actually."

"I'm sorry."

"Oh don't be sorry. It's you who's having the hallucinations. I just meant that here we are, surviving and we have a man down." She pulled out two vacuum packed rations from her satchel. "Now, I don't know what time it is but you should let me treat you to dinner. Soy or pork?" she asked with a wink.

19

— . —

Thea, although bone-tired, stood on the shore, holding her shawl tightly. The wind felt bitter and heavy against her body.

Her hair, untied and uncombed, blew excitedly directionless in the breeze as she looked out into the horizon: a flat black line across a light grey sky and even greyer sea. The wet air stung her skin like the salt of tears. She stared aimlessly at the vast, black ocean laid out before her. Her bare feet were entrenched in the cool, sinking sand. Cold, icy sea water tickled her toes and enveloped her ankles, gently pulling her back out with it. Once, she had felt the instinct to lift her feet out of the sand and move back; she didn't feel the need to do that any more.

She had cast a glance at the pebbles leading up to the sand dunes and wondered how many of them she would need to fill her pockets with. She felt that she would go out with the tide and never return, wondering if there was a limit to human emotional endurance and assumed that if there was, she had reached it within a single afternoon of reading her father's journals.

She did not know how long she had been standing there; she didn't care, either. The tide dutifully erased her footsteps on the trail behind her as though she had never been there to begin with. Thea, for the first time in her life, was able to make a safe exit, should she wish to do so.

Thea thought of the mirror image that shone down at her from the surface of the rock pools she had passed to get to the sea. She wondered if her dreams had been a message all along. Did it matter if she chose the sea instead?

Gulls cried overhead and dipped in and out of the glittering gunmetal depths. A small crab sidled up to a mermaid's purse, freezing momentarily every time a curious gull cast a shadow overhead.

The refreshing whispers and hisses of the water and the wind offered a strange sense of comfort to her, as though sirens waited beyond her line of sight, rolling under the waves to cloak themselves from the predatory nature of the human. The sun, as low as it was, pushed its way through the thick, silver cloud, warming her body with its narrow rays.

"You've always loved coming here." Her father's voice came from behind her. She turned to see Derrien bending over and picking up a shell. "You wanted nothing more than to beachcomb when you were a little girl." He held the little shell in the palm of his hand and wiped the wet sand off its ridges. "You always wanted to be a beachcomber." She turned away from him again and wiped her tears with the back of her hand.

"The little girl wanted to be a beachcomber," she sniffed, looking at him over her shoulder and then to the shell in his hand. He held it out to her. She took it from him and studied it, rolling the shell across her fingers. "This had been a limpet. So dependent on everything else and here it is, a hollow shell." Her finger and thumb rubbed against the smooth, white, shining interior.

"You remember though, don't you?"

"Not really." She shrugged. "I can barely remember being a little girl." She thought of the little girl in her dream, collecting things along the shoreline and stuffing them into a little bag. She saw her now, skipping along, singing to herself and playing in the waves. She stopped to look at Thea with a curious tilt of the head. Her hair was the same as Thea's: red and wavy albeit more tangled. Her eyes were the same blue but appeared bigger on a smaller face. She waved to Thea with a smile that revealed some distinguishing missing teeth appropriate for her age. Thea gently raised a hand to wave back. The little girl skipped into the waves and vanished from sight. Thea watched in disbelief and blinked. "At any moment now you're going to reveal to me that I've been living under an enchantment," she said quietly. She was looking at him again. He hadn't seemed to notice the girl. "You're going to explain what's going on. You're going to tell me why I suddenly woke up from years of sleep and felt alive for the first time." She looked him dead in the eye. "You're going to tell me why this has happened."

Derrien took a deep breath. "I think you know why."

"I want you to *tell* me." She dropped the shell onto the sand. "I need to hear the words come from your mouth."

Derrien stared at her, unable to speak. His eyes were glassy as he bit his top lip.

"Tell me it was all a dream. Tell me I'm imagining it." Her eyes filled with tears. The anger was rising in her voice. "Tell me it's not real."

He said nothing and instead, looked into the distance. "I can't tell you that."

"You will tell me what I have a right to know." She squared up to him. "I have a right…" she held her hand to her mouth. The sickness in her stomach lurched but she suppressed it with deep breaths. "I have a right to know."

"Thea–"

"Please! You've lied to me all of my life. If you love me, you'll tell me the truth." He opened his arms and she fell into them, sobbing into his shoulder. He held her there for a moment with tears falling from his own eyes. His bottom lip trembled uncontrollably.

"I did what any father would do," he said. "Please understand that."

"You murdered Shona Lennox."

"You understand why though, surely?"

"I do," she sobbed. "But it doesn't make this right."

"It doesn't," he agreed.

"How long have you had this power?"

"Since… since after Shona's death," Derrien said. "It grows stronger every day." She pulled away from him and readjusted her shawl, studying his face. "I feel that I am no longer in control of it."

"Promise me that you won't harm them."

"But they deserve to—"

"No, father. They don't. You know that this is madness."

"For what they did to us?"

"What they did was wrong," she began. "But I think you have tormented them enough."

"It will never be enough," he snapped. "They sent us out here to die, Thea. Marooned in this strange place. Shona lost her mind, Thea! She tried to kill us all." He ran his hands over his balding head. "She poisoned the drinking water! Do you know how long it took for me to fix that? She wanted us all dead." He brushed what little hair he had back, away from his shoulders. "She let her husband throw himself off those cliffs, there. He fell prey to the madness here and she did nothing. She did *nothing*." He looked at the looming, dark sky. "She didn't care who lived or died and she needed us out of the way. She wanted all the power for herself."

"It wasn't like that," Thea pleaded. "She was trying to protect us. Shona was your best friend–"

"Don't you tell me what Shona Lennox was to me," he scowled. Darker clouds began to roll in, bringing with them taller, fiercer waves. They crashed against the rocks with a deafening break. Thea stepped back slightly in subservience.

"She said there were more of R.E.L's kind coming. She said they'd kill us all and she was lying. She lied so we'd let her kill us. She tried to kill *her own son*, Thea." His voice was loud and carried across the sweeping winds, echoing off the cliff sides. Thea looked around in bewilderment. She did not recognise the man who stood before her. The spray from the sea spat in her eyes as she tried to keep her focus on him. "I had to protect my family!"

"You don't know that my uncle tried to kill you."

"Why else would we be here, Thea?"

"Please," she grabbed his arms. "Please let them go."

The raging winds grew stronger, chasing the gulls away with a nip on their tail feathers. Thea struggled against the wet sand holding her feet in place and felt that she was the only creature left on the beach, cowering in the shadow of her father. "They will never leave this place," he vowed. "I will not allow it!" Lightning crashed against the trees on the clifftops; smothering them helplessly with flames that oppressed them into blackness. Rocks slid from the edges of the cliffs and crashed into the sea. Thea wrapped her shawl around her head, attempting to secure the strands of hair that whipped her eyes in the wind. Black clouds swirled into a cyclone above the island.

"And what of me? Can I go?" she shouted. Heavy, pelting rains thrashed against their skin. Despite her fear, Thea stared hard into her father's face, approaching him slowly. "Or would you kill us both, too?" He did not seem to hear her. She waved her arms in frustration. "Kill us both too then!" Her rage consumed her, bubbling in her gut and pulsing through her veins. She pushed him backwards with a cry.

His eyes rolled back into his head and he fell to the ground with a sudden loss of consciousness. Thea, on seeing that the waves were coming in to claim his body, dragged him out of the shallow waters and over to the sand dunes. The dry sand flew in all directions, blinding her and choking her as she attempted to breathe. "Stop it, father!" she cried. "Stop this now!" She shook his slack head and shoulders violently on the sand. She could not hear if he was breathing over the howling winds and heavy rain. "Stop it!" she screamed.

His body sat bolt upright immediately as he took a shuddering deep breath. With his exhale, the clouds instantly dispersed, taking the rain and wind with them. The tide was dying back. He groaned and held his head in his hands. "Shona had the power," he said matter of factly. His wide, dumbfounded eyes found Thea. "It drove her mad."

He thought of the moment he came into the garden and saw Shona, right before he strangled her in a rage. He remembered her bulging eyes and hanging jaw. He wept into his hands. Thea stood over him.

"If this power is what you say it is, we need to leave," she said, removing her shawl and tying it around her shoulders. "How are we going to get out of here?" She thought of Geraint's shuttle at the bottom of the loch. She didn't know how deep it was but she suspected it was a lost cause. She started to panic.

"I have a ship," Derrien said quietly.

"What?"

"I have a ship. An old one. It's hidden in the caves."

She grabbed him by the collar in a fury that surprised her most of all. "You have had a ship this entire time..." she hissed, "and you didn't *tell me*?" He looked at her with large, sad eyes. Despite herself, she pitied him immediately. "The father I had once looked up to is dead," she said with a hollowness in her voice. "This pathetic excuse for a man is all I have left to work with." She let him go gently.

"We have a ship. We can go now. Right now," he said, clambering up to his feet.

"No." She held up a finger to silence him. "Not right this second. I'm not going anywhere until you let the others go," she said sternly. "And I'm not going anywhere without Jet."

"Thea, Jet... he..."

"What?"

"He'll never be able to come with us," Derrien said, rubbing his temples. The late afternoon sun was glowing from behind the light cloud now. The wet sand shimmered with long streaks of white tide-marks. The gulls coasted overhead on the calm winds, shrieking in delight.

"He can," she said indignantly, "I will speak with him. I can tell him everything." She helped him to stand.

***

Journal of D. Victor Smith- August 10th, 2306

God forgive me. I had to do it.

She could not be helped. I took her neck in my hands and I crushed her windpipe like it was a paper straw. Life and death and everything I thought I knew about it, disappeared. She nearly killed me. I stare at my hands every day. It's as though it wasn't me who did it. It wasn't me who did it.

The Derrien I was is not the Derrien I am now. This environment has demanded change. She will forgive me.

Shona Lennox always was and always will be my best friend. I miss her face. I miss her jokes, I miss the way she teased me and knocked me down a peg or two, but I stood over that Shona's body and I was glad she was dead. She became a monster. The witch is dead.

Forgive me. I do not mean to speak ill of the dead but she tried to kill her own son. She very nearly did! Fine, kill me and Thea but her own child? Her own flesh and blood? I would never do that. I couldn't let it happen, either.

It's just me and Thea now.

Jet is gone. He doesn't know the truth. He wouldn't listen. He's somewhere out there. He'll have to come back when he can't find his own food.

20

—·—

Jet led the party through the jungle, bounding tirelessly through the brush and parting dense shrubs to make way for the strangers. They followed quickly, not wanting to lose him or themselves again. Even with reassurance such as the familiar sounds of wildlife, the jungle had been hostile and difficult to navigate.

During their rest at the nearby camp, Seb had been able to repair his scanner and track down their shuttle, Callisto. He had given the coordinates to Jet and – as much as it worried him to learn– Jet knew exactly where the shuttle was.

"You know this jungle well, then?" he asked.

"Like the back of my hand," Jet replied.

Seb found the young man's expressionless face unsettling. "The guy never smiles," he had whispered in his report back to Owen.

"Who are we to judge? It's a miserable place," Owen had said, remembering back to recent events. "Keep your guard up, anyway." It was Owen's nature to give anyone he met the benefit of the doubt. "He's probably just as wary of us as we are of him and he has a right to be."

Jet was indeed wary of them all. Accustomed to spending most of his time alone, fighting with Derrien occasionally and only having Thea to talk to, he was not much of a conversationalist in new company. Several times, the eye contact he made with the others felt awkward and accusatory. He decided to walk at the front and keep speech as limited as possible. They could think what they liked, he thought.

Seb had continued to eye their guide with a quiet suspicion. If Jet knew he made them feel uncomfortable, he didn't show it. He approached every task with a monk-like focus, mostly saying nothing if he could help it. With Seb's help, the stretcher was constructed in a matter of minutes. Seb could not recall having ever met a person with such rapid problem solving skills. The strange young man was a marvel. "We could really do with someone like you on my team," Seb said. Jet looked at him, unsure of how to respond. Seb raised his eyebrows, "of course, only if there's nowhere else you'd rather be." Jet stared into the flames with his trademark, serious expression. He had never thought of leaving since his mother died.

"Leave this?" he asked, sitting back in a squat. Seb looked at him for a moment until Jet broke the pause with a wry laugh. "There's an easier life out there, right?"

"Much easier, probably."

Jet thought about the work that was demanded of him in order to survive on Oceanus and looked down at his calloused, rough hands that were heavily tanned. Seb's hands were almost like a woman's hands to him, with long, white fingers and clean nails, even in a damp, earthy jungle. "What's your job?" Jet asked him. Seb straightened slightly, as though surprised at the sudden question.

"Mostly security. I'm Owen's assistant, but I do other work some-times."

"What like?"

"Anything that pays well. You'd be a good fit for some of the stuff I have to do." Seb looked around at Owen, Geraint and Ade while they worked on their tents and shelters. They hadn't heard him. "We're always looking for skills like yours."

"I'll think about it," Jet said, looking back into the orange flames.

***

For the hours that they waited for the rain to stop, Seb had rested with one eye open, always watching and waiting. The jungle was unbearably humid, with warm droplets of water worsening what Seb thought was an already-overwhelming sensation of clamminess. He was rudely awakened from his catnap by the guttural barks of howler monkeys echoing overhead, followed dutifully by the squeaks and squawks of the macaws.

"They sound worse than they are," Jet remarked with a smirk. Seb looked over to him. "They sound awful, don't they?"

"Oh, yeah," said Seb. "What are they?"

"Howler monkeys were those loud barking sounds. The squawking is Hyacinth macaws. Ever seen them before?"

"No." Seb thought of the old files on Earth and its jungles. "I think they all died out on Earth."

"Is that where you're from?"

"Nah, I'm from Mars."

"No jungles there?"

"Nope." Seb sat back on his elbows. "Where are you from?"

"Here."

"Born here?"

"No, I'm from somewhere else, I guess. I just don't remember." Jet tossed some more kindling into the fire. "My family are all dead."

"Oh. I'm sorry to hear that."

"It happened a long time ago," Jet said, snapping more twigs.

The two men sat in silence for some time, wiping the drizzle from their faces as it trickled down from the dense canopy overhead. Jet felt himself strained with silence by the time Owen approached them. "Would you say the rain has lightened enough, Jet?" Owen asked. He looked refreshed, notwithstanding the recently acquired scruffy stubble on his jawline. "I'd like to get them as soon as is possible."

Jet looked up at him and nodded, seeming relieved. A longtime creature of solitary habits, he was comfortably out of the spotlight now. Seb's attention, although at first welcomed, left him feeling like a bird in a cage; he didn't know why.

***

As was expected of him, Jet led the rescue effort, guiding the sling down with ease. They did exactly as he said, pulling Anthony out first and laying him on a stretcher. He was heavy and half awake but Ade checked him and encouraged him to take more medication immediately. Trin, being half the size of Anthony and a strong climber, had proven to be much easier to retrieve. Notwithstanding her physical and mental exhaustion, she pulled herself up for the most part; as Owen had observed, she was almost in tears with relief after receiving a helping hand or two.

Unlike the others, Trin did not eye Jet with suspicion. As was her gift, she seemed to always see the positives. "Thank you, *so much*," she had said to the stranger earnestly, shaking his hand. He didn't have to give it to her: she took it with minimal resistance. His hand felt rough and huge compared to the smaller, softer one that grabbed his as though it belonged to an old friend. Her demeanour sparked his interest immediately, forcing him to exchange his aloofness for intrigue. She was not like the others.

"It was nothing," he shrugged, "but you're welcome." Trin stung him with another friendly smile and returned to Anthony's side.

"We'll have to find the shuttle today," Seb said to Owen as they trudged through the jungle. "Half my tent is under Anthony's arse."

Anthony, fatigued from another night of hardly any sleep and another helping of hallucinations, lay on the makeshift stretcher in a semi-conscious state. His skin, ashen and clammy, emphasised the dark rings under his eyes. Seb, Ade, Trin, Geraint and Owen carried him, sharing his weight. "I can walk, you know," he grumbled, looking up at the sky with disdain.

"Let's wait 'til we get to the shuttle," Trin said with her trademark smile. He looked up at her and wondered how she did it. How, even when they'd had to sit in a cold pit covered in mud, was Trin still smiling? Despite the compulsion to rant, he couldn't bring himself to do it. The very presence of Trin Rowan was disarming. "I'd really love a cup of tea," she said with chattering teeth and an unapologetically open yawn. She looked up and down the length of the stretcher and added, "I wouldn't say no to a lie down either."

"I've had enough of lying down."

"Anthony," Ade cleared his throat, "that sedative was enough to stop a giraffe from walking for the day. Take it easy."

Anthony sighed and rested his clasped hands on his chest in defeat. His clothing was torn and damp, he was tired and weak and his mood was rotten with a familiar glumness. "I think I'm losing my mind," he mused.

Trin looked at Ade nervously.

"You'll be all right, Anthony," Ade said. "There's something about this place that seems to trigger hallucinations in some people. It could be a hallucinogen in the air, perhaps? I don't have all the equipment and I'm going with my gut, of course but it would explain a lot. I think we're all losing our minds, in one way or another."

"Don't say that," Trin said, quietly.

"That's my only theory, anyway." Ade shrugged. "No one's been the same since we got here."

"Geraint," said Owen, changing the subject with a heavy breath. "Tell us about how you landed." All eyes were on Geraint.

"Oh, I don't really remember." He felt his skin flush a betraying shade of crimson, burning through his cheeks as he smiled nervously. "I think I must have passed out in the shuttle."

"Was it just you in the shuttle?" asked Anthony, finding a second wind.

"Yes. I was asleep when the alarms started," Geraint admitted.

"Funny, I can barely remember landing now. I know it was only two days ago but it's been a long two days at that," Owen said, looking at Geraint. The sight of his only son once again thrust everything into his face for reconsideration. Owen reflected on everything they had been through as a team and everything he had experienced not just as a leader but as a father, too. He had felt the sense of loss and grief and the agonising fear that he had lost his son to a strange world. The malevolence of the jungle and Anthony's hallucinations had depleted any energy reserves he had left, leaving him tired and wanting nothing more than to go home. *Stuff The Rimar*, he thought to himself. He had his boy back.

"Tell me about it," Anthony sighed, "I swear they're trying to kill me."

"But you're feeling better now, aren't you?" asked Trin.

"I am, yes. Thanks to you nagging– sorry, keeping me awake." Trin scoffed and shook her head. He thought that the crown of frizzy curls graced her face like a golden halo. "Seriously, that soy was to die for. You know how to treat a patient."

"Have you been having any more hallucinations since coming out of the pit?" asked Ade.

"No. The last one was in the pit."

"Good. What about you, Geraint? Did anything happen to you while you were out there?"

"I... actually, yes." Geraint felt that if looks could kill, he'd have been obliterated into the ether by the concentration of eyeballs fixed on his face. "When I was on my way here to find you, something was breathing on my neck, following me." He thought of the tight grip and wondered if the bruise was still there. Something had been able to touch him but he couldn't see it. "It... It was strangling me by the time I told Jet about it. He couldn't see it but he believed me... It stopped, anyway. I put it down to fatigue."

There was a pause as they each looked at one another.

"It's not just me, then," said Anthony.

"Anthony, I did just tell you this," Ade said.

"Oi, I told you I'd seen things, too. I thought Geraint was dead," Owen added, looking down at Anthony who was sulking in the stretcher.

"I suppose you did, yes," Anthony admitted with a raised eyebrow.

"It's weird though... how it doesn't happen to all of us, isn't it?" asked Seb. "Or maybe it does and we aren't aware."

"We *all* got lost in the jungle and somehow ended up in that pit without falling," Ade said.

"You know, it felt like one of those dreams," Trin began. "One of those times when you dream you're putting your foot through a hole or a puddle. Your stomach drops and you jolt awake. I remember it feeling like that! Do you?"

"Yes, actually," said Seb, taken aback by the description. They all nodded in agreement. "We came back to our senses but were actually *in* the hole."

"The pit felt as real as anything," Owen said. "I can't begin to think of how we got in there. I'm just glad we got out."

The tension among the group was palpable. Each felt that their mind had been violated but not by each other. Something else took the privacy of their dreams away from them. "Call me crazy but I think we're all being messed with," Trin said, looking at Anthony once more. "By someone or something."

Owen glanced ahead at Jet who was powering through the trail as though he knew exactly where they were going. "None of us know why this happened and none of us know why we're here in the first place." His eyes met with Geraint's. He had not told anyone beside his son about Derrien Victor Smith.

Their resigned silence was interrupted by Jet as he gestured for them to follow quickly. "I've found it," he said.

They picked up speed and hobbled along in Jet's shadow. The young guide bolted ahead and started removing palm leaves and debris from the battered shuttle.

The vessel was deceptively large enough for the crew of five, with a flat roof and portholes– none of which were damaged. Although dented, it had the appearance of having only just landed. Owen, at the sight of the red stripes and the markings denoting a familiar name: *Callisto*, sighed a breath of relief.

21

2 295- Atlantis

"Come in," Gene Lewis said, tidying his desk. Derrien opened the door and stepped in. "Ah, Derrien. Thanks for popping in." Lewis stood up to shake his hand. "You look tired. Sleeping ok?" Derrien took Lewis's frail hand with a firm grip. His hands would not betray him today.

"Not really. Is it a surprise?" Derrien asked, slumping into the chair opposite his colleague.

"I'm sorry to hear that. How is the medication?"

"It's better than nothing," he said. He hadn't taken a sleeping tablet in weeks. The last box was still full, waiting in his medicine cabinet at home. Derrien preferred to take a dose of *nothing*. *Nothing* hurt more. *Nothing* reminded him that he was still alive.

"How is the little one?" Lewis asked with a smile. Derrien looked over at a framed photograph of Lewis's grandchildren that graced his desk. Three happy faces looked back at him. "She's fine. Still asks for mama but... what can you do?" He fought back tears and swallowed hard, fixing his red-eyed gaze on Lewis.

"I'm so sorry."

Everyone was sorry. Derrien felt he had never met so many sorry people in one place. Even the people he had never met were sorry. Sorry did nothing for him but he nodded and thanked everyone all the same. "So, what did you need me for today?" he asked, desperately wanting to change the subject.

Lewis leant back in his chair and clasped his hands together. "There have been some...comments about your latest thesis."

"Regarding?"

"The androids. I have them here." Lewis picked up the report from his intray and began to read. "Language shows sympathy toward the androids involved in the Lisbon revolt. Sympathy expressed towards androids. Unapologetically biased towards... androids. Expressing admiration for the ingenuity of synthetics. Dangerous ideology." Lewis sighed. "You get the gist."

"Are these all separate complaints?"

Lewis indicated that they were. Derrien shook his head. "You know, I always knew this would happen. Start thinking along different lines to our great benefactors and you'll get yourself in trouble."

"I don't know what you mean."

"Oh come on, Lewis. How else is this little utopia doing so well? They flush the bad ideas out as soon as they get a sniff of them. All I said was that the uprising of 2118 was indicative of human behaviour."

"You likened them to those who rose up to... hang on, I've got it here– the Haitian revolution of 1791?"

"And?"

"They were machines, Derrien."

"They were slaves."

"My word. Just listen to yourself!"

"Slaves. What's wrong with that? Did we not build them to enslave them?"

"We built them for service, yes."

"But they were enslaved. We were fine with it until it got too expensive. No one has been worked to death like that since the twentieth century. The trawlermen stopped returning, the miners collapsed in the pits, the construction workers couldn't manage the tools, the pleasure units started crying during sex–"

"Derrien!"

"Slaves."

"Derrien– you can't enslave something that has no self-awareness."

"But the Beckmann report of 2050 suggested that everything that lives has will of some scale. It even suggested that most creatures that live have some form of self-awareness."

"They were animals. These are machines–"

"The Khan report of 2115 revealed that not only were these synthetics *alive*, they lived in family groups."

"What? Where did you–?"

"You can get anything on Mars for a fair price. There are perks to it being the shithole of the galaxy– you can sell everyone's secrets to gain some status."

"That's nonsense."

"In 2160, the Brazilian government reported that they'd found a colony. Escaped androids built it deep in the Amazon rainforest. They'd mutilated themselves to remove their tracking chips. The journalists–who conveniently went missing afterwards– followed the marauders, found a fucking crib and children's toys. No kids had been reported missing for the first time in fifty years. What would androids want with a crib and a bunch of toys?"

"You've gone mad. That's hearsay."

"It's sitting in the archives of the Martian Library of Human History. But you're right, it must be nonsense. Lisbon and Jakarta were just glitches."

"They're machines, Derrien."

"Quote the party line all you want. If they were machines and simply machines, why did they wake up one day and think "I'm being oppressed by humans," –where did they even get that from? Their consciousness gave it to them. Here's a theory: God creates man, man creates android, man decides that android is a living, hideous reflection of themselves, so man destroys android. They smash that mirror and they bury it! Those machines think and they feel and that's why we had to wipe them out. We don't like that about them. Jakarta was the most peaceful revolt since Ghandi told India to down tools. We slaughtered them because they did not behave as we *wanted* them to behave. We've tried time and time again to just create something that cannot think for itself but the creator always forgets one small detail: we make everything in the image of ourselves. Christ, even the housefly has free will. I don't know why everyone gets so pissy at the thought of synthetics being human in all but name. It was inevitable! The sex bots were fun but they weren't *real* enough. The punters wanted them to be more *real*. All of the investors wanted workers they could smack around and hopefully, those workers would sometimes– to their delight–try and fight back. 'Make it more real. Make it more real' and they got what they asked for, didn't they? Synthetic genes, synthetic organs, synthetic hormones, synthetic life: real cruelty, real exploitation, real suffering, real death."

He thought back to the reports he'd read about cruel, powerful men found stuffed in the laundry chutes of their mansions. Theories suggested that housekeeping had finally had enough. Every single bone was broken from the impact. He thought of the photographs of crippled, defaced synthetics living in the gutters of some of Earth's wealthiest cities, no longer wanted. "Make it more real," he said to himself with a breaking voice.

Lewis stared at him, raising his top lip in disgust. "What's got you into this?"

"This whole place is a lie, Gene. We're monsters. We've done awful things to own paradise and I can't live with it. The truth needs to be told."

"It's not the truth, Derrien. It's a conspiracy."

"Everything is labelled a conspiracy until it's proven to be true."

Lewis, finally out of patience, rolled his eyes. "God, this is nonsense."

"All right. It's nonsense. It's just a theory. The trillionaires colonised space, brought prehistoric mammals back from extinction and finally— ended hereditary illness forever, but something as simple as androids having consciousness is *nonsense*? Why am I being called in to discuss something that's just 'nonsense' as you put it?"

"These are dangerous thoughts, Derrien." His tone lowered to one that was more serious, more threatening.

"Ah! There we go. The thought police of Atlantis want to speak to me. I am disrupting the peace!"

"I think you need some time off."

"I don't want any."

"You're showing signs of…" Lewis started to fumble around for the button under his desk, maintaining eye contact with Derrien as he did so.

"What? Madness?"

"I wouldn't put it like that."

Derrien leaned into the desk with a penetrating glare. "Say it."

"I think you're having a breakdown. It's perfectly understandable, Derrien–"

"Oh fuck off. You don't understand."

"Derrien, please– I'm trying to help you."

It was dark by the time Anthony tried the door of the campus AI lab. It was locked. He knocked. "Derrien, you in there?"

Somewhere behind the locked door he thought he could hear the sound of metal sheets wobbling. "Derrien?" Anthony asked again. He knew that his brother was in the lab. Not only had the security guard told him where Derrien was but the personnel scanner revealed that Dr Victor Smith was indeed, downstairs in the lab. Anthony had visited Derrien's home first and on discovering that the babysitter was still there, hurried to campus to find out why his brother was working, when he was on strict orders to stay home and rest. "I know you're in there," he said, gently trying the handle one more time.

He fumbled around in his pockets for his government-issued master keycard. "I'm coming in," he declared, swiping the card. The light around the lock flashed green and unlocked the door.

"Couldn't you hear me?" he asked, looking into the room. He clocked Derrien quickly covering something in a cloth sheet.

"What have you got under there then? A dead body?" he joked.

Derrien froze.

Anthony pulled back the blue sheet.

"What have you done?"

22

—·—

S eretse Walner, the captain of the S.S Demeter, was a man in his late forties and– as far as people from the colonies were concerned–a rare native of wealthy South African Earth. Balthazar, a Martian, had always been envious of Earth's inhabitants, especially those living on the African continent. The captain was an anomaly. Walner, despite coming from a country that– as far as Balthazar knew–financially propped up Earth and, by extension, colonisation of space with its wealth of natural resources and tourism, served as captain of an envoy ship, hundreds of millions of miles away from home. Balthazar, wanting to ask him *why*, always held back and imagined an exciting scenario instead. The fantasies were wild. Perhaps Walner did something scandalous and took a job in space as a way of saving his reputation. Perhaps, he fell in love with a visitor from one of the colonies and followed them back to the frontier. Whatever story Balthazar cooked up in his head, he still didn't get it. Why would such a privileged man from Earth come to space?

Walner was funny, professional and approachable but even so, Balthazar understood the basics of command and knew 'the captain isn't a friend,' as his father had warned him, several times. Once, when they were departing for New Botswana, he laughed a little too hard when the captain said, "New Bots is just like old Bots... but shit."

Balthazar had never been to Botswana. He would probably never be able to afford to, either. Captain Walner was the closest he would get, so he clung to him like a captivated child wanting to hear another story about lands far from reach.

He wouldn't have been the only Martian to feel this way. There were people on Mars who–given the chance–would sell organs to live on Earth, had there been any need for organ donation on the planet in the twenty-fourth century.

With Balthazar's help, the Europa had travelled back to the Demeter with a strained Captain Walner, an unconscious co-pilot, a frightened navigator, a rattled engineer and an exhausted communicator. The only person able enough to help him get his ship back up and running was Balthazar Swaine, Cabin Steward.

"Swaine? You did all this by yourself?" the captain asked, looking over the ship's log and status reports. The familiar hum of the machines and cool breeze from the air conditioner soothed him as he looked around at the consoles and lights. "You don't know how nice it is to get some functioning lights for once," he said. "I need to see how everything is working and then we can relax for a minute."

"Aye, sir."

The captain pulled the blueprint of the ship onto the screen and activated the SITREP update. "Ok Swaine, how are the engines?"

"Seem to be working, sir, but I'm no engineer so I couldn't switch them on or anything."

Walner nodded. "Fair enough. Damage?"

"None that I know of."

Walner sat down in his chair, watching the screen for any anomalies. "I need to know the current status of the uncategorised."

The *uncategorised*. That had been the first thing on Balthazar's agenda when he opened the shuttle bay for the captain. In his mind, he had hoped they were on the brink of an exciting, life-changing discovery and Balthazar Swaine, certified ship's idiot, would be part of it. Successfully suppressing his tendencies to blurt out or impulsively start on a new activity, he had instead greeted everyone with a smile, readying the medical bay for the crew.

"They're here, sir," Balthazar said, pointing to the co-pilot's screen on the bridge. The white lights stood still, almost on top of one another. Beside them was a solitary red light. "One has moved since I last saw this screen."

"Mhm," Walner said. He held his chin in his hand, brooding over the data. "Is this red one one of ours?"

Balthazar shook his head. "I'm not sure, sir."

"Well, six are back on here. Six are next to the Callisto... but we can't be sure who." Walner leaned back and placed his hands on his knees. "Ok, here's what we're going to do... we're all going to take the Lisbon test. No one comes back on the Callisto until they've– oh–"

The SITREP report had finished, revealing several areas for review. Walner opened the notifications tab and inspected them. "Cause of damage to the shuttles... ion storm. Another ion storm on the way. Should be here in an hour."

"That's not enough time to get them back, sir."

"No, it's not," he agreed, sitting upright. "We can get a message to them. It shouldn't affect them on the ground– it's just too dangerous for launch and entering orbit. It'll cover the upper atmosphere and cut communications for a while. Once it passes, they can launch." He stood up from the console. "Tell them to do the test and find shelter– just in case. It could be another twelve to twenty-four hours before they can come back... luckily, the Callisto isn't damaged."

"And the uncategorised, sir?"

Walner fixed his eyes on the white dots. If he was worried about the uncategorised, Balthazar couldn't see it in his face. Instead, he could only see that his captain was coming to a decision. A deep crease set in on Walner's forehead. "They're not going anywhere by the looks of it. I've seen this kind of thing before." He noticed that Balthazar was staring at him, wide-eyed and, not wanting to stir up a frenzy, waved his hand dismissively. "No, no aliens or synthetics or anything like that. It was just a couple of turtles, believe it or not."

"Oh, I see." Balthazar's shoulders sank. He felt that his dreams of discoveries were shattering before his eyes. "Could just be some reptiles. Of course. I should have thought of that. Reptiles."

"Maybe. Reptiles are good at that kind of thing. The crocodiles in Bots are a pain for fooling the perimeter scanners." He shook his head. "We've gone through many pet dogs as a result. Anyway, let's just review it over the next twelve hours. If they've been here for the entire time that we have, the threat level is low. Just tell the crew of the Callisto to test, find shelter and approach that part of the island with caution. I also want a status report on their welfare. I hope they haven't been through anything like what we've had on the Europa; Quinn was seeing things from the moment we landed; Ahmed is worn out, Jessops is unconscious, and Jorgensson is the only person on board with medical training. We're in dire straits, to be honest with you. I'll get us a cup of tea and check on that lot downstairs," he said, swiftly exiting the room.

"Aye sir." Balthazar typed in the clearance code and opened a channel to the Callisto. "Oo, wardroom wets. I must have done all right," he said to himself.

23

— · —

T rin wiped another cluster of damp, tightly ringed curls from her forehead and sighed. "I need a shower," she complained. "A waterfall will do. I can't stand this humidity any more."

Anthony, lying on his side on the bed, looked across to her. "You're not a fan of the regency look?"

"Not right now, no," she said, exhausted. "How are you?"

"I've been better. I think I'm feeling better though, you know."

She seemed relieved. "That's good."

There was a knock on the shuttle door followed by Owen's head. His hair, usually a short, tight-waved display of salt and pepper, was lank and flat. "How is everyone in here?"

"Fed up."

"Fair enough. I'm just going to check the comms system again," he said, brushing past them to get into the cockpit. He closed the door behind him to allow for his tall frame to enter. Trin watched with keen interest as the door slid open again.

"We're going home soon," he said quietly.

"When?"

"There's an ion storm coming so we have to wait another twelve hours or so but the captain is back on board and will pick us up as soon as it passes."

"Amazing."

"I'd better tell the others, but there's something else." He seemed embarrassed—nervous even. Trin looked at him searchingly. "Grab a Lisbon kit from the medical cabinet, please. We need to test."

"It's one of us. It must be," suggested Ade with a gentle shrug. Tired and defeated, the doctor could have believed anything at that moment.

"This is ridiculous," said Anthony from the doorway of the Calliope.

"I know but we won't be able to go anywhere until we test," Ade said. He held up his hands. "Listen, this is less than ideal but we want to go home, don't we? The message says there are two uncategorised life forms among us. They could both be androids..." he stayed silent for a moment, looking at the troubled faces around him. "Or something else. The test will take a blood sample, a fingerprint and a retinal scan. If any one of us are synthetic, we only need to fail one of these things. If any one of us are aliens, we'll fail all of them." Ade forced a smile. *Aliens*, he thought. *That would be the cherry on the cake.* "It'll be ok. I don't think there's anything to worry about, but we can't get back onto the Demeter unless we pass the test." At 43, Ade had been in the medical corps for over 20 years. In those years of near-catastrophic breakouts, chemical attacks, disease screening and scandals, he could not recall ever having had to use a Lisbon kit to test for alien life. He fought with every shred of will available to him to keep his hands from shaking.

"The doctor's right," Owen said, splashing his face with some water. "There is no one in this party that I don't trust, but the Demeter detects that there could be a synthetic or even an alien on the island with us and we can't let it board if so." He looked reassuringly at

Geraint. "We'll be back on the ship tomorrow morning... tonight, even."

Synthetic. The word stirred up more emotions for the team than *alien* did, which– to Owen–sounded ridiculous. He wanted to laugh.

Seb couldn't stop thinking about it. He had heard many rumours about synthetic parts on the black market, but he'd never heard of a fully functioning synthetic. On the one hand, the thought of being in the presence of one gave him sickening chills; on the other hand, he felt a rush of curiosity and excitement for what was about to happen.

"But," Geraint held up a hand, "what if it's someone on the island? Will we just leave them, or..."

There was a thick quietude, smothering them for a moment. Owen rubbed his chin and looked at Seb. "We will cross that bridge when we come to it," he said with a forced smile.

"I'll go first. I have nothing to hide," Geraint said. Ade nodded and opened the test kit. The box clicked open automatically, presenting the test tubes, paper and needle. Geraint held out a hand.

As the others stood around watching, Trin and Anthony– from their seated position in the doorway of the shuttle, looked at each other, "You know," she whispered. "I would still fancy you if you weren't human."

"Trin, that's not funny," he whispered back, more seriously than he had intended. "Anyway, I saw you eyeing Indiana Jones over there." He nodded his head in the direction of Jet, who stood with his arms folded, watching Geraint complete the test.

"What?" she half laughed. "He's barely twenty."

"What's wrong with that?"

"I'm thirty-nine, Anthony."

"Christ, really?" He regarded her for a moment with raised eyebrows and smiled. "Maybe you're the synthetic," he teased, patting her knee. He winced as he felt the sharp twist of his nipple. "Sorry, sorry," he said with his arms raised. "You can't be, you're right." He rubbed his chest slightly. "A synthetic would have ripped that off."

Surprised at themselves but at the same time, understanding that it was probably due to the irrationality of the setting, they both giggled in the corner, covering their faces while Ade assembled the kit. "I've just realised something," Anthony whispered.

"What?"

"You've stopped calling me sir."

"Oh sorry—*sir*," she said sarcastically.

"Like that, is it?"

"Now isn't the time," she said, blushing and looking away. Anthony stayed silent and turned to watch the show, thinking about her words while he did so.

Seb carried a tray with the instruments while Ade prepared the needle and paper. "They know it's not me. You can't give one of these IV drips to an android, and an alien... well, an alien would probably need it up its... you know, bum or something." Anthony pointed to the cannula in his forearm. For as long as he was required to use the drip, he was pinned to the shuttle.

"You're still getting the test, pal," she said, patting him on the hand. She looked at his tired face. His eyes were heavy and sunken. "Maybe you should get some sleep, too."

He gave her a regretful grin. "I don't think that's a good idea."

His eyes, usually protected by a semi-permanent furrowed brow or a scowl, were open and vulnerable. Trin stroked a stubbled cheek with her finger. "It'll be all right. We'll get to the bottom of this."

He thought of the horrors that waited for him in his dreams, with their snarling teeth and sharp fingernails, plunging their serrated edges into his skin. His heart was growing tired of the repeated shocks, aching in his chest. "I hope so," he said.

They watched Ade prick the tip of Geraint's finger first. The droplet of blood fell into the glass tube of clear fluid. Ade inserted the paper and waited for a few seconds. It turned blue, as predicted. "It would stay clear if you were a synthetic," he said, turning to look at the others. He then held the scanner to Geraint's eyes. It hovered for thirty seconds, shining brightly, narrowing his pupils. It beeped and a green light flashed on the scanner. "Just a finger print now into this putty," Ade said, holding out the small pad for Geraint's finger. It encased the fingertip for a few seconds and shrank away. Geraint breathed a sigh of relief. "Congrats, you're human!"

He did the same for Seb, Owen, Trin and then Anthony. Jet was the last to be tested before Ade.

There was an unspoken, lingering notion that if any of them were to be more than they seemed, it would have been Jet. Jet could feel the mistrust in the camp when he volunteered his own finger to Ade. There was an audible sigh of relief among the onlookers when his blood, fresh and red, turned the liquid blue like the rest of them, and his retina generated a green flash from the scanner.

When it was time for Ade to do the test, he gave the apparatus to Owen and held out his finger. Owen carefully carried out the test as instructed by the doctor. The silence grew heavier for a moment, weighing everyone down.

"Thank god for that," Owen said. "It's no one here." Trin almost clapped.

Jet and Geraint exchanged a look. Jet, feeling the familiar sensation of his heart dropping through his gut and into the void, said nothing and looked away.

24

— · —

A tlantis, 2296- 15 years earlier.

Derrien stared at the plant that held court from the edge of the coffee table in the centre of his hospital cell. His bed, neatly made, lay across one wall, with a sofa and entertainment console occupying another. He glared at them from the other side of the room, having vowed not to use them in protest. He imagined that he was watching a production from the stalls, or a doll house from an armchair. At any moment, the play would begin.

His fantasy was interrupted by a gentle knock at the door.

"Come in, it's not locked," Derrien said, sitting on the floor. Anthony stepped into the room.

"How are you?" he asked, trying to sound upbeat. The sleeves of his heavily creased shirt were rolled up, revealing dark patches under the armpits and around the collar. He looked like he hadn't slept in days.

"How do you think I am?" Derrien scowled, focusing on the shiny, leather shoes on his brother's feet.

"Come on, Derrien," Anthony said, despondent. "You need to show progress or they won't let you out."

"How's Thea?"

"She's fine. I've asked Jane to do bed time but I read her a story before I left."

"Good. She likes her stories."

"She does. She would like to come and see you. Do you want me to arrange it?"

"No. I don't want her to see me like this. Daddy looks like a criminal."

"It's been six months, Derrien."

"She can't see me like this."

"She just thinks you're in hospital."

"Good. Tell her I'll be home soon."

Anthony threw his head back and rolled his eyes. "You *would* be home if you showed some progress."

Derrien looked at him, clueless. "I've done nothing wrong. I'm perfectly sane."

Anthony's heart sank. Every night they had this meeting and every night, Derrien refused to see what everyone else could see. Anthony finally snapped. "I've got to ask *why*, Derrien? Why did you throw it all away?"

"Why does our dark history not move you?"

"It was all unfortunate."

"Anthony, you read my thesis, didn't you?"

"Of course I did."

Derrien's eyes widened. "You made the complaints, didn't you?"

Anthony almost fell back into the wall with the weight of the accusation. "No! Absolutely not."

"My more handsome, more charming, more socially acceptable brother might worry about his own career if his brother writes a thesis like that. It's understandable, Anthony. But you can't have Thea, too."

"What?"

"I know you want her for yourself. You seem to have it all but you don't have a child of your own. No worries, you can just take mine! You just want her for yourself, don't you? That's your plan."

"Derrien, please, I'm begging you to–"

"You wanted Cara, too. I know you did. I saw the way you looked at her."

"Fucking hell. You're getting worse." Anthony ran his hands across his face and into his greasy, dark hair. He looked even more tired than he had before.

"My eyes are open now, that's all," Derrien said. "I see it all now."

There was another knock on the door. Anthony shot a wild look at Owen as he entered quietly. Owen, oblivious to Anthony's panic, headed straight for Derrien and squatted down opposite him. "Derrien, I'm sorry that we are in this situation but..." he looked up at Anthony. "It's been too long now and I have to make a decision. How about we do a deal?"

The small, inconspicuous shuttle was waiting for them in the unlit cargo bay. "I've managed to get some of your things from your office but it isn't everything," Owen said apologetically. Derrien opened the door and peered in. There were a few boxes and some of his personal belongings stowed away inside.

"Why are you doing this?" Derrien asked, raising a thick eyebrow.

"Anthony asked me to help you. Your only choices are a complete digital wipe and a penal colony, or you can go away with these papers and start again somewhere else... I couldn't have one of the greatest names in science destroyed. Can you imagine the uproar from the community? This is the best I can do for you, Derrien...but you must promise not to revisit the work you've done here. You have to start again. Do something else. Get into botany or, I don't know... farming.

I've got your papers here." He handed him a wallet of documents. "A new identity." Derrien took it from him but didn't look at it.

"But why are you helping me?"

"Look," Owen said, putting his hands in his pockets. "I've known Anthony for years and well, he never asks for anything. He asked if there was anything we could do for you. This is what I can do."

Derrien opened the wallet and flicked through the papers. He saw a new birth certificate, citizen card and academic achievements. "Where are Thea's documents?" he asked.

Anthony breathlessly jogged toward them. "We don't have a lot of time," he said. "We have no business– You need to go before the power comes back on."

"What about Thea?"

Anthony and Owen looked at one another. "We thought it best if Thea stays with me." Anthony said with a sorrowful glance. "It could be dangerous."

"She's my daughter."

"She's my family too, Derrien. I don't think it's safe for her to–"

"You bastard!"

Derrien lunged at him, punching him across the face with his chaotic fist throws. A lucky blow caught Anthony's cheekbone and sent him reeling backward. Owen quickly grabbed Derrien and pulled him off. "Derrien, we have to do what's best for Thea!" he barked. "Come to your bloody senses."

Derrien resisted for a few moments more before he shrugged them off him. "Fine, I'll go. You're murdering bastards. I could die out there." He eyed them wildly. "Just you wait."

"This is the best we can do for you... for your reputation, Derrien," Owen said, holding his hands out.

Without a further word, Derrien boarded the shuttle and closed the doors, turning his back to them. They stepped back and waited for him to start the engine.

***

Owen dozed, listening to the rhythm of erratic knocks and buzzes. The red numbers on his bedside clock beamed into his half-closed eyes. It was three o'clock in the morning. He sat up, listening for the knocking again. It persisted. His wife, Adrienne, slept soundly beside him as he gently climbed out of the bed and descended the staircase.

The knocking grew louder as he reached the porch. Through the peephole, his bleary eyes could recognise the familiar face of Anthony. He quickly unbolted the door.

Anthony stood on his porch with his hands on his knees, panting.

"Thea's gone," he said, crumpling into a sob. "He took her."

"What?"

"He took her. They're both gone!"

25

--·--

"That's it then. Time to leave," Owen said, almost feeling the warm sun of Atlantis on his face as he said it.

"Wait—what? What if there *are* androids?" Seb asked.

"What if there are?"

"Shouldn't we check it out?"

Owen shrugged. "We haven't been asked to. We're not a research team."

"But they could be just here. There could be two. Aren't you tempted?"

Owen regarded him for a moment. He couldn't read Seb's expression. "Of course I'm tempted. I'm as tempted as Icarus was tempted to fly a bit closer to the damn sun and this is why I'm going home." He turned to walk away.

"They could be dangerous," Seb suggested.

"They could be, aye," Owen agreed, "but this isn't our jurisdiction and I think we've suffered enough, don't you?" He nodded towards the shuttle where Anthony was still hooked to the drip. Seb shrugged.

"What if whatever it is comes after us?"

Seb held his breath and watched the seed drop as intended in Owen's mind. What if it did come after them? Owen paused for a moment, thinking of the next step. "Seb, load this stuff into the shuttle," he said, pointing to their camp. Seb silently obliged. He watched Owen approach Geraint. "Geraint," Owen said to his son, "come with me."

***

They walked some distance to the outskirts of the camp. Owen looked over his shoulder and began to talk in a lowered voice. "Is there an android?"

"I don't know," Geraint said with a shrug.

"Are you sure?" Owen looked into his son's eyes and frowned.

Geraint, unable to lie to his father or to himself, shrugged. "If there is... I think it's Thea."

"What makes you say that?"

Geraint thought of the kiss and how cold she seemed to him. To the touch she felt as warm as anyone but he couldn't forget the stare– the alien expression on her face, the questioning of his behaviour and the unfiltered bafflement. He couldn't forget the way she was so eager to serve her father– something he had never seen before. She was incredibly beautiful, cheerful and kind but there had been something about Thea that kept her at arm's length from him at all times. "She has to be," Geraint said, sadly. "But wait— you won't hurt her, will you?"

Owen's eyes rolled back. "Son, why do you always do this?"

"No, it's not like that– she's kind, Dad. She's kind. She cares for things."

"You know what we have to do, son." Owen turned to walk back to the camp.

"You don't," Geraint pleaded, grabbing his father's sleeve. Owen stopped abruptly. "You can't hurt her. She's as real as you or I. She'd never harm anyone. I mean– for god's sake she dived into a loch and pulled me out. She saved my life, Dad."

Owen studied the boy's face for some time and saw genuine concern. "She's a friend of yours?"

"You could say that. I owe her my life. The shuttle I was on sank. I wouldn't be standing here now if she hadn't pulled me out."

Owen exhaled all of the tension in his body and shook his head. "How am I going to explain this when the law is very clear?"

"The law is for soulless robots, Dad. This girl is something else. She'd never hurt anyone."

Owen raised his hands in protest. "Son, we're talking about an android. It's just a robot. Pre-programmed to do as it's told. After Lisbon—"

"Thea's not like that. She wouldn't hurt anyone."

Owen couldn't believe what he was hearing. The synthetic had a name. He stared at the boy as though, by some misfortune, they had entered a parallel universe where the synthetics *did* win the sympathy of mankind. He sighed again with a deep frown. "You're sure?"

"As sure as I am that *you* wouldn't hurt anyone, yes."

Owen's stomach, bearing a dull heaviness, ached as he thought of Derrien Victor Smith, his little daughter and the shuttle they fled on. "It's got to be the girl," he said. "This isn't Derrien's first android, Geraint."

Geraint turned pale. His father sat down against a tree and invited him to do the same. He let out another deep sigh and rubbed his forehead. "I told you I knew him. I told you that he used to live and work on Atlantis. I told you that he's Anthony's brother. I didn't tell you what he did, exactly."

"You told me that he violated the Paris convention."

"He did, but I didn't tell you how. When Professor Cara Tate died, Derrien was devastated. The scientific community was also devastated. He was held in incredibly high regard, you see, as a man of science and a real visionary. An expert on AI defence technology— there was nobody like him. He was a genius— but none of us were prepared for what Derrien would do out of grief and madness." Owen paused and looked up at the treetops for a moment. Geraint watched him intently, hanging on every word. "Anthony found it. He was working on a new project. An android of all things... he created an android of Cara."

Geraint focused hard on his father's face, tracked the movement of his mouth and allowed the words to land in his ears but he couldn't hear them. Owen observed the blank expression and nodded. "Yes, you heard me." His eyes were heavy, as he said, "he made a synthetic of his dead wife."

"What? But Lisbon—"

"Yes, I know."

"This is pretty bad, then?"

"You could say that."

"What happened to him?"

"Well, he didn't stand trial because we covered it up." Owen let out a shallow laugh, "that's the first time I've told anyone." He rubbed his temples. "Nobody knew except for a couple of colleagues, Anthony and myself... and now you. He had a kid, for goodness sake. She was around your age... I couldn't have her father wiped, imprisoned and then come home to look you in the eye every night." Owen thought for a moment, "but, hang on... if she— where's his kid?"

Geraint, realising what could have happened, slumped down against the trunk of the tree he was leaning on.

"Derrien is... I think he's dangerous," he said.

"He probably is. He's probably got another android in a shed somewhere in case that one malfunctions."

"Seriously?"

"I don't know. There are two unknowns. I'd bet he's responsible for both of them."

"Dad," Geraint whispered.

They heard a twig snap. Owen crept around the tree and looked out into the clearing. He returned to Geraint silently. "You're the only one I can trust, son," he whispered. "Follow my lead."

***

Owen and Geraint returned to camp having agreed not to say anything about Derrien for the time being. They boarded the Callisto as instructed. The storm was looming over the upper atmosphere, east of the island by the time they had activated the engines. Ade and Seb piloted the shuttle while everyone else huddled around the makeshift sickbay, secured as well as possible. Jet, having never travelled by shuttle in living memory, held on tightly to the support rail, trying not to look out of the porthole beside him.

The equipment rattled with turbulence as the vessel hovered above the trees. Jet thought he was going to be sick.

"Here, put this on." Trin leaned over and handed him a travel band. "Slip this on your wrist there," she pointed to the acupressure point on the inside of his wrist. "It's an old method but it works. It stops you feeling sick."

"Thanks," was all he could manage before she had to hand him a paper bag.

Geraint, looking out of the porthole on his side of the vessel, thought about the circumstances that had brought him to Oceanus. He could barely remember it but he was certain that there hadn't been a seatbelt involved. He held onto it like a lifejacket, sliding his fingers across the strap to make sure that it was still there. The nausea he felt– nothing to do with turbulence– forced him to look down at his feet. He jumped slightly when a hand– his father's hand, touched his shoulder. "Won't be long now," Owen said.

"Owen, what's waiting for us down there?"

"I don't know," he began. "If what I've learned is true, I know what we're about to meet. I'll see, but I don't know anything for sure. You should all stay here in the shuttle until it's safe to come out."

Owen noticed the look of concern across Trin's face; he felt that had Anthony been awake, there would have been a name on the tip of his tongue, too.

"I simply mean with the storm being dangerous," he said, pointing to the ceiling. "I don't think the uncategorised will harm us." *I'm actually worried that there's a psychopath down there*, was what he wanted to say, but he remained calm and collected. "It will be ok."

"How do you know?"

"The captain doesn't know for sure but he said in his message that, going by probability, if there's anything else here, it's likely not harmful, whatever it is," Owen said. "Cold-blooded animals often come up as *uncategorised*, you know." He gave her a wry smile. "But saying that, prepare yourself for anything."

Trin seemed placated and folded her arms, looking over to Anthony who had been sedated again against her wishes. Ade, after observing a correlation between fear and the hallucinations, decided it would be best for all if Anthony was asleep during the journey. Owen had authorised it. Trin, unable to do anything, stayed by his side. Although she outwardly gave the impression that she was relaxed, she was no longer smiling.

Owen glanced down at Anthony's peaceful face with a pang of envy, as his friend lay there, oblivious to all of the chaos that was about to unravel around them. He hoped that, by the time he could explain his partial dishonesty, Anthony would be understanding.

***

Derrien was waiting for them outside of the sandstone cottage when the door of the *Callisto* opened. He felt a rush of nerves come over him as he looked at it, lowering down onto the ground. Part of him wanted to chase them away– frighten them, even; the other needed the company.

Jet, on seeing his face, took a deep breath and stayed seated, as did Geraint and Trin.

Owen, as agreed, had been the first to leave the vessel. He raised a long leg and secured a foot on the first step. "Stay here until I tell you to come out," he said to the others, patting his filthy, creased uniform down with his hands. "I'll handle this." He held on to either side of the doorway and tentatively descended down the stairway.

Derrien watched him with folded arms. He did not know how to look at a man he'd been banished by and hadn't expected to see again, so he stared.

Owen met him with a similar bearing, but held his palms open at his sides. Blood was pulsing in his ears, his throat and the rest of his tired body. He inhaled all the air around him and straightened when his feet stopped at the foot of the ramp.

"Hello, Derrien," he said.

26

— · —

"**I**s my brother with you?" Derrien asked, looking down his nose.

Owen nodded, thinking of Ade's report on Anthony's heart. "But we can't let him see you. He's seriously ill, Derrien." Ade had warned that Anthony's heart had endured too much stress for such a short period of time and, without a hospital or an organ lab nearby, his next shock could be fatal.

"Pity," Derrien said with a scowl.

Owen, pretending not to notice Derrien's remark, pointed toward the house. "I think we should go inside and talk, don't you?"

In a moment that could have been a brief hallucination, Owen's eyes swiftly moved from Derrien's face to the female form that had just emerged from the doorway of the cottage. His heart stopped. She stood on the doorstep, barefooted and divine. If Owen hadn't been at her funeral, he'd have tricked himself into thinking it was Cara– alive and well. The blue eyes were set in the same way, with a small, freckled nose and long, auburn waves cascading down to her waist. Derrien followed his line of sight and looked back at Owen. "This is Thea," he said, irritably. "You remember my daughter, don't you?"

Owen could not speak. Derrien sighed and turned toward the cottage. "Bring them in. We'll make some tea."

Inside the cottage, the warmth of the fire was welcomed by the travellers. Trin warmed herself while sitting on the floor, rubbing her knees as they returned to their natural colour. The others sat where they could find a seat. Thea silently brought them a tray of tea and toast.

Every person in the room found themselves unavoidably charmed by the tragic beauty that walked among them, handing out cups and plates. Trin noticed her eyes most of all. They were deep pools for any wandering soul to find themselves lost in. She thanked her for the tea and toast and returned to facing the fire.

Ade, trying not to look too closely at her, thanked her nervously for her hospitality, taking his tea with the most unsteady hand that he– a doctor– had ever operated with. Seb's expression was one of amazement. He did look. He looked for too long.

Derrien sat in the armchair in front of the window, cross legged and prepared to talk.

Trin gulped her tea down greedily and gnawed on her toast while Owen studied his host over the top of his cup, trying to wet his mouth as quickly as possible. He barely recognised the top professor in AI defence technology sitting across from him now. Derrien had wilted, somehow. Owen felt that he was no longer looking at a man but a sun bleached tuft of a dead plant.

He watched Thea gracefully leave the room and return to the kitchen.

"So," Derrien began, "you've come to talk. Let's talk." Owen looked around at the others and saw that they were still like statues. "Don't worry, they can't hear you. It's just us for the moment. I'm a bit of a wizard around these parts." Derrien winked.

Owen smirked, retracting it quickly when he realised that Derrien was deadly serious.

"What?"

"It's a thing. I'll tell you about it someday but for five minutes or so it's just us. Anyway, fire away."

"How long have you been here?"

"Since the day you packed me off in that shuttle. Surely, you remember it well."

"I thought you were dead."

"That was the plan, wasn't it?"

"Never."

"I don't believe you."

"I promise you– that was *never* the plan. We gave you papers to start somewhere else. You couldn't *be* Derrien Victor Smith any more. I still remember when the remains of the shuttle returned to Atlantis. For the rest of my life, Derrien– Anthony's too– we had to live with it. We had no idea what had befallen you and Althea. To this day, I assure you, I am sorry. So, very sorry."

Derrien remained silent, realising that the shuttle had returned on a boomerang route. "Surely, if the shuttle returned, you could have tracked its journey?"

Owen shook his head regretfully. "It was badly damaged. The log was empty and there was nothing inside that could have indicated where the shuttle had been. Highly unusual, I know, but you must believe me. I know it's of little consolation but we-we gave you a new life– free of scandal."

"Scandal. You're one to talk."

"We spared you," Owen snapped. "What you did could have started a war. Decades of peace and promises of AI disarmament and you go and pull a stunt like that!"

"I was grieving."

"As were we all. Cara was a wonderful woman in every respect, but that doesn't give you a right to play god."

"That was different."

"How so, Derrien?"

"I just wanted my wife back. I wouldn't have bothered anyone."

Owen blinked several times. *Wouldn't have bothered anyone* replayed in his head. He gripped the arms of the chair he was sitting on and drew a slow breath.

"I can't believe you. You're not that stupid. You know as well as I that once that technology was alive and kicking, we'd be thrown into chaos. Of all the colonies I'd suspect of dabbling with androids, I didn't think it would be ours. How could you have been so stupid?"

"I was grieving."

"And this time?"

"Same reason."

"What?"

"Thea died, Owen..." Derrien said in a low voice, stunning Owen into an open-mouthed stare. His face, previously unconcerned and haggard, reddened as he looked into Owen's eyes. "She was poisoned to death and I– I had to bury her. She was ten." He began to cry. "She wouldn't have died had we not come here. It's your fucking fault. Yours, Anthony's, Atlantis... all of you are complicit because I wouldn't be here if you hadn't put me on that shuttle."

"Derrien, I'm—"

"No," he said, brusquely holding up a hand. "It is what it is. I still have a daughter... but she's not the Thea who died."

"Does she know?"

"I would assume that she does, yes."

"How long has she been operating?"

Derrien, hurt at the prospect of Thea being described as *operating*, chose to shrug it off. "Since she was ten. She can remember back to being ten."

"Why did you do it?"

"I did what any of you would have done given the chance," he said, staring into the fire, frozen in time like a painting. "Look how far we've come and still, the parent can outlive the child. It will always be a crime of the universe. When you find your only child choking from poison that someone else– someone you trusted— administered, come and judge me. When you lay your only child to rest on some isolated planet, then, come and judge me. I've driven myself mad thanks to you and pictured how my revenge would play out every single day. You sit there on your high horse quoting law to me but you know what, Owen? It was *that* Thea who told me revenge wasn't the answer." He pointed to the kitchen, where Thea was standing still. "It was *that* Thea who said I shouldn't kill you. You have that girl to thank. You think she's just some-some–machine but she gives more of a shit for humanity than I ever have– I'll tell you that."

"She is a machine, Derrien."

"She's not. She has a soul."

"Derrien, this has been done before. They do not have souls. They are not conscious like we are."

"Lies... and you know it. The Mendelson report of 2185 revealed, Owen, that all living creatures have choices. Free will isn't a bad thing. Even the common housefly has free will. Does that make it a killer? No. You have free will." he leaned in to look closely at Owen. "Are you a killer?"

"She needs to be deactivated, Derrien."

"I'll kill you all before you touch her."

"You know the Paris convention, Derrien. It's outlawed."

"No laws here," he said defiantly. "I can do what I want outside of the boundaries. Shona Lennox did and no one came for her. She was a murderer, you know." Derrien looked over Owen's head to see Shona standing by the lake, watching them.

"I don't know who that is."

"That lad you've got with you– Jet. His mother. Top scientist sent here on a terraforming mission. They cancelled the project and ordered everyone to evacuate. Crazy bitch came back with her family on her own terms. Nobody bothered to try and catch her." He folded his arms and sneered. "Shona was human, Owen. Shona was a murderer. That girl in there though? She wouldn't hurt anyone."

"She needs to be deactivated, Derrien."

"No. Who are you to take her soul?"

"Who were you to give her one?"

Derrien eyed him sternly. "You touch her and you can kiss goodbye to your ship."

Owen felt his body sinking deeper into the chair, holding him there, making him listen. He eyed Derrien. "What will you do?"

Derrien tilted his head back with a chuckle. "What *wouldn't* I do? How do you think you came to be here?" he asked, shaking his head. "It was me, of course."

"How?"

"I had help, but I can get what I want."

"What help, Derrien?"

"I think you have your suspicions. Go on, I'd like to hear them."

"I don't know what you mean."

"Come on, Owen. The hallucinations? The storms? You don't think that was simply chance, do you? The nightmares that keep you on your toes?"

Owen felt it, too. The presence of something that wasn't within sight, but all who walked on the island felt it. An ever-present, silent stalker, playing with their minds. It was in the room with them. "What is here with us, Derrien?"

"I'll tell you if you promise not to hurt Thea."

27

The room had returned to normality in the blink of an eye, characterised by the crackling fire that breathed heat into every corner. Derrien, flushed, addressed the others, "I see that you have some questions that need answering."

Owen, still glued to the chair– his face pale with fear– felt like a mouse whose tail was still tangled in the claws of the cat, waiting for it to start the next round of games. Derrien wielded a power he had never seen before and– to Owen's dismay– would use it at will with no fear of consequence, like a bear defending its cub. Owen, looking away for a moment at the brooding grey sky outside, resolved to tread lightly.

Inside the landed shuttle, Jet, who had volunteered to stay with Anthony, watched his charge for any changes in behaviour. He had been warned of Anthony's hallucinations, but keenly offered his help nonetheless. While the others went inside for refreshments and food, Jet thought of Thea. He hadn't seen her since she told him about the survivors. He had been grateful for the distraction, but now the dust started to settle, presenting him with embarrassment and awkwardness. His face was hot, and he didn't know how he'd be able to look at her without remembering her pushing him away. The words she said still circled around him, taunting him. As Jet pondered, looking out of the porthole, Anthony started to stir.

"Where's Trin?" was his first groggy question. He looked around the shuttle, desperately searching for her.

"She's gone inside for a minute."

"Inside where?"

"Inside the cottage. They needed to talk to Derrien." Jet immediately felt himself turn cold, his stomach dropping at the slip, remembering that Anthony wasn't to know anything.

"Talk to who?"

"Um, th-the guy who lives there. There's a storm coming and they need shelter."

"Derrien."

"What?"

"Derrien. Is there a bloke called Derrien in there?"

"No."

"You said Derrien."

"No, you misheard me."

"So if I go in there, it'll just be a Derik?"

"No, you're supposed to stay here."

"Piss off with that." Anthony shot up and pulled the drip out of his arm, setting the monitors off on a shrieking campaign. He stumbled to the floor and pulled himself up again.

Jet tried to sit him back down but Anthony overpowered him. "Please get out of my way, lad," he said quietly.

"You're supposed to stay here," Jet insisted, holding him down.

Anthony heaved himself up again, out of Jet's arms; Jet tumbled to the floor, crashing into the medical apparatus. Like a caged animal breaking free, Anthony marched out of the shuttle, rolling to each side of it and landing with a smack like a drunk, clambering up and grabbing the rails. Jet leapt after him but it was too late.

"Derrien? Derrien! You come out here," he cried, standing before the cottage.

The cottage door opened slowly. Derrien's eyes met with his brother's for the first time in over a decade. Anthony, unable to take the shock, clenched his chest and gasped for breath before his world went dark.

***

Seb watched from the sitting room window of the cottage as they scrambled together to resuscitate Anthony, who lay there on the ground, limp and lifeless. His torso jolted up and down as they pushed and pumped, scurrying for the defibrillator and aid kit.

Seb stepped back from the window and took a steadying breath. He felt that there hadn't been a better opportunity to have a look around the cottage and find what he was looking for. He had nosed around upstairs when he'd used the bathroom earlier. The drawers were mostly predictable: underwear, notebooks, hairbrushes, and jewellery. He rummaged around the kitchen, checking under counters and tabletops for keys or devices; nothing was evident.

His last resort was the hallway. He passed the front window again, checking to see if they were still outside. They were all surrounding the shuttle now; he had some more time.

On entering the cottage earlier, Seb had caught sight of a second door in the hallway. It had a keyhole underneath the handle but to his amazement, it wasn't locked. He opened it and stuck his head into the semi-darkness. It was a staircase to a cellar. He closed the door behind him and slowly made his way to the next door at the bottom. Again, much to his benefit, the second door wasn't locked either. "What are the chances?" he asked himself quietly, wiping a sweaty palm on his trousers. The door opened with ease into an empty, clinically clean room with monitors, filing cabinets and machinery that he wasn't sure what to call. His shoes squeaked against the polished tiles as he tiptoed over to the main computer.

He fingered his way through some files that were sitting around on the desk and pulled out a parcel tube. He popped the lid off and took out a roll of paper. It was a large drawing of some sort. "Bingo," he said, studying it. It was the blueprint of the Galileo. "Now, if I just had a — oh my god." On the wall opposite him was a giant map of the island. He recognised their current location instantly and where they'd been. He traced the map with his finger and landed on a point of interest. It was an underground hangar. He ran back to the main desk and searched for a pen and paper.

Another book fell to the floor and from the inside of it slid out a few more pages of graph paper. They caught his eye immediately.

"No fucking way."

He couldn't believe his luck. The diagram he was looking at was titled "Thea." He stuffed the plan back into the notebook and secured it into his rucksack with a firm tug of the zip. He checked it again, to ensure that he had closed it properly and held the bag tightly to his chest, guarding his treasures.

A faint noise caught his attention. It sounded like a deep thunk followed by bubbling. He hadn't noticed that there was another door at the back of the room and even in light of the unlikely opened doors, he looked at this one in bewilderment. The door before him was unremarkable save for a metal plaque bearing the letters R.E.L. The noises he could hear were coming from within.

Seb looked down at the bag and back at the door again, wondering if the universe was setting him one more challenge. If he turned away, he already had indescribable riches in his possession. If he investigated further, he thought he would be in with the chance of finding more.

He tried to lift his hand to meet the knob; he was suddenly overcome with a paralysing anxiety that he couldn't place, which seemed to cause it to shake uncontrollably. He fought against his instincts and tried to touch it one more time. Just as he lowered it to grasp the round, cold brass, he had an overwhelming compulsion to let go, turn around and leave the room. His head throbbed: brainfreeze. He darted out of the lab and closed the door securely, sensing the pain lessen with every step he took towards the staircase. He quietly put his rucksack on and held onto the handrail.

Hearing footsteps upstairs, he followed silently, steadying his excited breath. When he felt it was safe to, he opened the door at the top of the stairs and crept back into the hall. He peered through the window of the sitting room to see that everyone seemed to still be outside. Everyone except the bonus prize. He stalked her footsteps into the kitchen and pounced.

She had no sense that he was coming, nor could she leverage herself to fight back as he covered her mouth and held a blade to the small of her back. "Come with me and don't say a word."

28

—・—

T hea cried out as her head made contact with the wall of the hangar. The pain almost blinded her as she lay still, weeping. The warm trickle of blood from her forehead slid down into her left eye. As she tried to adjust her position, she realised that her hands and ankles were bound, aching with the pooling blood either side of the uncomfortably tight ties.

"You must understand, girlie," Seb said, squatting down to meet her eye level. "It's nothing personal." He shrugged. "You're a synthetic, I'm a human. It was always going to cause trouble."

Her eyes widened. "Oh," he laughed. "You didn't know, did you? Well this is just awesome."

Thea felt that she had ceased to breathe as she listened to him talk. "Your kind are outlawed. Seriously, it would start an intergalactic war— you're so bad. That's why this all has to be done on the hush-hush. Anyway, we'd better hurry up and go."

Synthetic. She held onto the words he'd said. Her body confused her. Her heart, beating violently in her chest, told her that she was alive. Her blood, trickling down her face, told her that she could be hurt. The pain she felt in her body told her that she *could* feel. She was alive. He had to be wrong.

He dragged her by her ankles to the Galileo, hauling her up onto his shoulder as he approached the steps. In a manner similar to that of discarding a sack of flour or a rolled up rug, he dropped her against the bulkhead of the cargo hold. She whimpered when she banged her head again. He looked down at her and shook his head. "Actually, no. I need to keep an eye on you," he said, picking her back up and placing her down again in the passenger seat of the cockpit. His eyes, bright with sinister joy, projected his state of exhilaration. "You see," he began, "swabs on Mars like me... we don't get to build colonies, pilot ships or do any other shit the rich kids do. We have to make our own luck and you," he pointed a finger at her, "you're going to make me a fortune. It's like finding the winning lottery ticket on the floor and cashing it in, it really is."

She looked at him helplessly, her frightened eyes glassy with impending tears. Every limb on her body told her to freeze but somewhere deep inside, she felt the need to fight. She *wanted* to fight. Seeing that her face was bloodied, Seb swept a finger across one of her cuts and inspected the blood. "It's as good as the real thing," he remarked, wiping it away on her sleeve as though it would infect him. "I've heard X-genesis pays handsomely for contraband...but we're talking relics or body parts. I've got the whole thing– living and breathing. I'm a made man," he said, ruffling her hair. She tried to scream but he knocked the wind out of her with a hard punch to the stomach. "None of that. No one will hear you and it does my head in. Be quiet or I'll find your off button." He moved a hand down her body, forcefully pushing it against her crotch. "I'm sure you've got one. Maybe I'll find it later." She tried to kick him and missed.

As much as he reassured himself that he had the upper hand, her retaliation frightened him; worried that he wouldn't be able to silence her, he found a bag and secured it over her head. "Shut the fuck up while I learn to fly this thing."

Whether due to a lack of oxygen or a loss of blood, Thea collapsed in the passenger seat, limply hanging forward with blood pooling on her lap. She didn't hear the door open or the commotion that followed.

***

"Thea," a voice said over and over again. "Thea, please wake up."

She opened her eyes to see a familiar face. His kind, brown eyes– although framed with bruising, cuts and swelling–were open, searching for life in hers.

"Jet, is that you?"

"It's me," he said with unrestrained relief. She eyed him dreamily, blinked and wailed into his shoulder. He waited patiently, speaking softly, reminding her that everything was going to be fine. She would be safe, as far as Jet was concerned.

"He tried to..."

"I know."

"What happened?"

"He tried to leave anyway. Something about already having enough to get what he needed. The ship was torn apart in the ion storm."

"Oh. He was on it?"

"Yeah, he was on it... after we'd been explicitly told not to launch for twelve hours," Geraint added curtly. Thea blushed, not realising that he had seen the whole encounter. She was still leaning on Jet, who held her close to him. "Madness, really," he shrugged. Thea found Geraint's mild irritation amusing.

"Where is everyone else?" she asked.

"Oh they're back at the house. Geraint came with me to come and rescue you."

"How did you know I was here?"

"Derrien worked it out– but don't worry— he would have come but, er, he fell and snapped his ankle after two minutes. We had to keep going and leave him to the others." Jet buried any sense of a smile that was trying to surface at the thought of Derrien hurting himself. "Old fool," he muttered.

***

Between them, Jet and Geraint had carried Thea back to the cottage and laid her on the sofa. Geraint found some ice for her bruises and Ade bandaged her up. Derrien barged into the cottage, limping with his temporary brace. "Thea!" he called as he collapsed onto his knees at her side. He hugged her tightly. "I'm so sorry," he said.

"I'm all right, father. It's just cuts and bruises," she lied.

Derrien composed himself and turned to look at everyone else in the room. He fixed his glare on Owen. "How do I know Seb acted alone?" he asked, pulling himself up again. He approached Owen slowly. "How do I know you didn't tell him to do this?"

Owen, as much as he wanted to react angrily, held his hands up. "This was nothing to do with us."

"How do I know that?" Derrien hissed.

"I suppose you don't. You only have our word."

Trin and Ade looked at Owen and then back to Derrien, who was listening intently to something and nodding.

"Seb acted alone, Derrien," said Shona, who was standing at the back of the room. Owen, seeing that Derrien was looking over his shoulder, turned to see what the object of his attention could be. There was nobody there.

"Shona said Seb acted alone," Derrien said. Trin's eyes widened, flicking back to Owen, who was looking at Jet. The young man remained still, staring at Derrien in disbelief.

Owen smiled wearily. "Shona is right."

"She is. She saw the whole thing. Seb saw an opportunity, raided my lab and kidnapped my daughter. It had nothing to do with you."

"Father, you're scaring them," Thea said weakly, looking over from the sofa.

Derrien inspected the faces around the room and lowered his shoulders. "Sorry," he said, returning his attention to Owen. "Can we talk outside?"

***

They sat down on a bench outside the house.

"She means a lot to them," Owen said sadly.

"Of course she does. She's a person."

Owen thought about the fear he saw in Derrien's eyes when he couldn't find his daughter; he knew the same feeling too well. It was the fear of a father. "This really complicates things, Derrien."

"I shouldn't have brought her here. I know that." He wrung his hands together. "She'd have been safer with Anthony, just like he said."

It took Owen a moment to realise that Derrien was speaking about the daughter who had died. The first Thea. He sighed, "Anthony will understand, Derrien. I'm sure he would have done the same, had it been his child."

"He wouldn't. Anthony is the level-headed one." Derrien swallowed, thinking of the brother who had encouraged him to build a career in science in the first place. "He was the sensible one." He looked over to the shuttle and thought about him, lying there unconscious. *I was going to have you all killed*, he thought; the sickening guilt curdled in his stomach.

They sat in silence for a moment and watched Thea rise from the sofa, nodding and shaking her head at several intervals. She was limping slightly but from what Owen could see, she was insisting that she could walk. They watched Jet sit her back down and hand her a drink.

"He's a good lad– Jet," Derrien remarked. "His mother tried to kill him."

"What?"

"Yeah. Shona was having hallucinations. Drove herself mad. Said R.E.L was summoning others to come and attack Oceanus. Decided to kill us all first before we could suffer."

"That's awful."

"Thea drank the poison first. I managed to... I managed to knock it out of Jet's hand. It was the drinking water. I found her lying there, still as a fallen petal, only her hair moving in the wind." He gazed into the distance as he spoke. "Ten years old, Owen," his hands trembled. "I tried to rouse her but she was dead." His lips kept curling downward, wobbling as he spoke. "The froth had spilled from the corner of her mouth. I thought it had been a seizure at first but Shona– Shona told me *exactly*. Said it was the only way– my world ended right there and then."

Owen's throat tightened as he felt the hot sting of tears spilling from his eyes. Derrien hadn't noticed, and kept talking. "I had to stop her so I– I strangled her with my bare hands. My only friend in the world and

I had to do that. The boy—he didn't understand. I ran to the cottage as fast as I could and shook him. Asked if he'd drank the water. He hadn't. He tried to see her and I wouldn't let him. He ran off and I can only assume, found his mother. I just left her body there, after all. Little Thea— she, she's um—she's buried on the cliffs. I was so broken, Owen. I was so alone." He turned to look at the governor who wiped tears from his dirt-clogged eyes. "I did what any father would do."

Owen remained still, watching the people inside the house talk and laugh together. Thea laughed with them, looking to and from Ade and Geraint as they exchanged stories with one another. Jet, as solemn as he had seemed, was laughing too.

"I would like to tell you that I can make a case for her," Owen said quietly. "But I can't." He looked away at the loch as it mirrored the white flashes above.

"She's just a girl," Derrien said, turning to him.

"I know, and that's why none of this is fair."

29

More than twelve hours had passed since the captain's first message. Owen surmised that if the ion storm had passed, Captain Walner would be back in touch as soon as it was safe. Having yet to receive such a message, Owen instructed everyone to find a bed for the night. Derrien had been able to offer two beds and a sofa. Jet returned to his woodcutter's hut; Trin had offered to sleep in the shuttle with Anthony. Thea, still too restless to settle for the night, noticed that the light outside the shuttle was still on and brought Trin some tea while Anthony slept.

When she heard the knock, Trin opened the door of the shuttle with an expression of shock that was hard to soften. Thea noticed that she was wary of her, and placed the tea on the top step instead of in her hands.

"This will help you sleep," she said, bowing slightly as she retreated. "It's chamomile. I made it myself."

"Thanks," Trin said after a pause, sitting down on the step. She was wearing Anthony's jacket, pulling it across her chest tightly. The mist was setting in over the loch for the evening. A solitary moon gazed down at its reflection, casting an ethereal light on the water and all that surrounded it. Trin's teeth were chattering.

"Are you ok?" Thea asked.

Trin snorted. "Wow, I'm here with six other humans and the synthetic is the first to ask me if I'm all right. Brilliant." She realised what she was saying and shook her head. "I'm so sorry, I shouldn't have said that."

"It's ok. It must be strange for you."

"It is, to be honest. But I still shouldn't have called you that. It's not nice."

"It's what I am. It's just a fact." Thea shrugged and put her hands in her pockets, rocking back and forth on her heels.

Trin regarded her for a moment. If Owen hadn't told her, she sensed that she would never have known. The girl had only ever been kind to her and she felt monstrous for having feared her. "I thought Owen had gone mad when he told me," she said. "I mean, a lot of people *do* go mad here, apparently." She thought of Anthony's screams and Derrien's conversation with the imaginary Shona in the cottage. She held the warm cup in her hands. "I was taught that your kind were just machines; machines aren't capable of anything but service...but that's all up in the air now."

"I'm sorry," Thea said quietly.

"So you're Anthony's niece?"

"Kind of." She smiled with a shrug. "It's complicated."

"Yeah...so is he," she said, pointing behind her shoulder.

"He'll be all right. Father says they can grow him a new heart on Atlantis." She looked at Trin with the wondrous gaze of a child. "That's amazing, isn't it?"

"If you say so," Trin said, looking at the living, breathing synthetic that had just made tea for her without being instructed to.

"Anyway, goodnight." Thea bowed again and left the doorway of the shuttle.

Trin watched her go back into the cottage and looked down at the cup of tea in her shaking hands. She burst into tears.

***

Back at the cottage, Owen and Derrien were talking quietly in the walled garden, watching the fireflies hover above them in the moonlight.

"They all think it would be unfair to deactivate her. Given what has happened today, we can't run the risk of anyone knowing that Thea exists. Seb was going to sell her to X-genesis. Even if she was– and this is just an example– no longer living, her body is worth...well, it would end life as we know it. There's no planet she can land on where they won't scan her retinas. There's no vessel she can board without being detected. I don't know what we can do other than leave her here."

"I'll stay with her."

"You'll die here, Derrien. If what you've told me is true, we all need to leave. The line between reality and dreams is blurring. That-that *thing* down there... it will kill you, eventually."

"That other thing is dealt with. There won't be any more hallucinations. I can stay."

"Derrien, this place isn't fit for humans. We all need to leave."

"The boy won't leave."

"Why not?"

"I've known Jet Lennox for most of his life, Owen. He hates my guts but I'm the closest thing to a father he has and trust me– I know him. He's stubborn. He loves her. He'd never leave her here."

***

It was midnight by the time Jet heard a familiar, faint knock on the door. He slowly rolled out of the bed and opened it. Thea stood outside, silhouetted by the moonlight. He could make out the faint whiteness of two eyes and a smile.

"Can I stay with you? I'm a bit..." she raised her finger to her mouth in thought, unable to find the words.

"People'd out?" he suggested.

She nodded. "How did you know?"

"I'm people'd out, too."

Thea laughed quietly. "Thank you," she said.

He invited her in and closed the door behind them.

***

That night, Thea dreamed that she was walking across the beach with her father.

No waves crashed against rocks this time. No winds whispered across the grasses on the dunes. The shore was silent as though it held its breath, waiting for Derrien to speak. He was clean shaven, dressed smartly and much younger than she had ever seen him. She imagined that her father looked as dashing as he had done when he lived on Atlantis, all those years before.

"You know, we could spend millenia creating the perfect human but we'd never learn that imperfection is the core of what it is to be human," he said, skipping a stone across the calm sea. It had never been so still. "You are imperfect and I love you."

He gave a pebble to Thea who took it reluctantly. He nodded toward the water. She threw with a gentle flick of her wrist. The stone landed into the water with a resounding plop. She laughed despite herself.

"See what I mean?"

"Oh," she held her head in her hands. "Did you have to curse me with feelings?" she sighed, wiping away fresh tears. "I would have preferred to have been a machine."

"Thea was never a machine."

"I'm not her, father."

"Oh, but you are. You'll always be that little girl who collected seashells and showed them to me. You will always be her. There's nothing that can change that."

She imagined a very small Thea, huddling for protection in his arms aboard their shuttlecraft: a tiny, frightened child, estranged from her father. Derrian had never been the same man since. She looked at him now, watching his heart breaking for the fourth time in his life.

"Must all the women I love leave me?" he said with a faint wobble in his voice.

"I think I remember, you know," she said. "I think I have her memories."

"Good. I wanted you to have them. They make you who you are."

She looked back at their footprints in the sand and thought of how many miles they had walked across that beach. Her heart felt heavy.

"If I do have a soul, we'll see each other again," she half said to herself.

"You do have a soul, dear girl. You're everything you should be and more."

"What is it they say, 'cogito ergo sum'?"

"I think therefore I am."

"I think therefore I am."

"You will always be my greatest accomplishment."

"Because I'm an android?"

"No. Because you're my daughter." He held her in his arms.

"You have to leave me here, father."

"I'll never leave you."

Thea turned from him and saw the little girl smiling up at her, with shells in her hand. She took Thea's hand and they walked together, back towards the centre of the island. When Thea looked back once more to see Derrien, he had faded into nothing; waves of foam-crested water rolled in, pulled back and swept his footprints away with them.

30

T rin was the first to wake the following morning. She opened the door of the shuttle and wrapped a blanket around her shoulders, stepping down the stairway onto the shore of the loch. Anthony's monitors had hummed and clicked in a low, reliable rhythm all night. The sleep hadn't come easily but the white noise helped her to drift off for a time, refreshing some of her senses.

The scenery before her was breathtakingly beautiful, even when shrouded in white mist. The cool, damp air was a dramatic change from the insufferable humidity of the jungle. She stood on the stony shore of the loch and dipped a toe in; it was freezing cold, but she was still tempted to get in. She imagined what it would feel like to swim in the black water. She felt that the silence and solitude of the early morning loch would wash over her, relaxing her muscles and soothing her stress. She felt that she could forget everything, if she were to lie down on the water.

Something made her look at the lake for too long. She was met with the notion that, had the water had a voice of its own, it was calling to her from the dark depths. She shook her head and stepped back, rubbing the blanket against her arms. Whatever the notion had been, it soon passed, so she stood for a minute longer, watching the mist grow thicker as it rose from the water.

***

Further down the shore, Jet was surprised to have woken up alone in his hut. He brushed a hand across the sheet where Thea had slept; it was cold, but so was the air in the room. Early morning light filtered in through the screen and a chilling breeze swept in through the open window. He turned over. A few strands of long, red hair remained on his pillow. He smiled to himself and sank back into the bed, wondering when she was coming back.

He waited for some time until turning over to see an envelope on his bedside table. He recognised the handwriting; It was addressed to *Jeremiah P. Lennox.* His heart skipped a beat. With clammy hands, he tore it open.

Trin heard the erratic splashes first, followed by the screams. She ran down the length of the dock to get closer to the water. The cloud of mist was so heavy that she could barely see two metres in front of her. She heard Jet's voice, crying and shouting and turned on her heel, racing around the loch, looking for a way in.

When she finally found him on the shore, she saw that he was dripping wet and holding Thea in his arms. He was sobbing uncontrollably. Trin fell to her knees in shock; Thea wasn't breathing.

***

The men had agreed to arrange a pyre to lay her body on. Owen insisted that, in order to keep Thea a secret, all evidence of her existence had to be destroyed.

Ade, admitting that he knew nothing of synthetics and understanding that his investigation could produce no useful results, offered to test for a cause of death anyway, however, Jet assured him that her death had been by her own hand, for her own reasons. He felt for the letter in his pocket. Everything she had wanted him to know was folded up inside it. He swallowed back tears and set to work on the pyre.

Derrien shook with a red-eyed anguish, wantonly shedding tears onto his face as they laid her body into the row boat. The captain's message was replayed on loop in the Callisto. "The storm has passed. Please return to the Demeter. All passengers are to complete a Lisbon test." Trin climbed up and muted it. The captain could wait.

Anthony watched helplessly from the shuttle as they arranged the kindling. His heart beat in his chest, pulsing a different pain through him. They had been able to fit a temporary pacemaker thanks to Ade's ingenuity but he had been warned not to do anything strenuous. Being one of the strongest under normal circumstances, he volunteered to help; Ade wouldn't hear of it.

It was Jet who arranged her body before they pushed it out into the loch. Trin, having watched the whole ordeal, looked down at the cup she had been given the previous evening and cried heavily into Anthony's shoulder, grieving for a girl she hardly knew.

As Jet laid Thea's body down, each of the onlookers tricked themselves into thinking she was merely asleep; she bore the look of an angel engaged in peaceful slumber— her face, a picture of seraphic calmness. All it would take was a gentle shake or a kiss and the nightmare would end, Derrien thought. The end didn't come.

Jet had assembled some of her favourite flowers and scattered them around her hair. He nodded to Owen when it was time to light the fire. He pushed the pyre out until the water came to his waist, remaining there for some time, seemingly unaffected by the chill of the water around him.

She drifted weightlessly toward the centre of the loch, her body burning up into the sky. Ade, Geraint and Owen stood together outside the cottage, casting their eyes downward. Geraint let the tears fall freely.

Anthony pulled himself up and climbed down the steps of the shuttle. Trin ducked under his arm and offered him some assistance, which he appreciated. He asked her to let him go when he reached Derrien, who stood there, leaning on a crutch.

Without speaking, Anthony held out his arm and comforted his brother from the edge of the loch, rubbing his back as he crashed to his knees and wailed into his hands.

31

—·—

"It's nearly time, Jet," Derrien said, limping over to him. "Is there anything you want me to get for you?"

Jet looked at Derrien's swollen, red eyes and then down at Derrien's bandaged ankle and frowned. "I don't think so, Derrien."

"I mean I could ask someone else," he said, looking at his foot. "It's going to heal. I just need to go to sick bay... Do you want your books or...?"

Jet stared at the loch. The pyre had been reduced to ashes. Everything was gone. "I built one for my mother, too," he said, quietly.

Derrien had always wondered what had happened with Shona's body, but he didn't say anything– rather, he lost some sleep worrying about it.

"I know you had to do it," Jet said, turning to look at him.

"You do?" Derrien seemed small to him. Pitiful.

"Thea left me a letter."

"She left me a letter, too," Derrien said. "What did yours say?"

"That's between me and Thea."

"Understood."

"Look, Derrien," Jet began. "I'm sorry for–"

"I'm sorry too, Jet. I'm sorry for all this misery."

"I should have listened."

"You weren't ready."

"I'm sorry."

"I'm sorry, too."

For the first time in over ten years, they shook hands. A peace settled between them. "You're still an arsehole," Jet said. Derrien gave a wry laugh, despite himself.

Owen approached the two men on the shore. "Are you ready to leave?" he asked, throwing his bag over his shoulder.

***

Aboard the Demeter, Captain Walner and his recovering crewmen welcomed the returned passengers back with firm but relieved handshakes. Observing that the white lights had disappeared from the screen, the captain waited for Owen to explain. He gave a vague answer about reptiles. Walner raised his eyebrows and turned to Balthazar Swaine. "See? Slippery bastards," he said. All three men looked at the screen to see no life signs of any kind.

"I am sorry about Seb Mariner," the captain said. Geraint looked at Owen.

"It was a tragedy. May he rest in peace," Owen said solemnly. "The storm was quite deadly. I don't know what he was thinking."

Walner welcomed Jet and Derrien, although– these were not the names that Owen had introduced them as. Owen had already drafted papers for a fifty-year-old forester and his adult son who were in possession of work visas for a five year term in the New Botswana desert; they had lost their way after a crash. "A noble endeavour," the captain remarked. "New Bots needs some TLC."

Jet sensed that, on shaking the captain's hand—this was all a game—a performance. He could hardly believe his own story, and felt that no one else should, either. He played along nonetheless. His hand had been forced and he was leaving Oceanus forever. He had never been so far from home, and watched as they drifted further from the planet. It grew smaller and smaller until it became a speck in the distance, shrouded by stars and the black vastness of space. He could not comprehend that one day, Oceanus would become a distant memory, embroidered onto a patch on the long, colourful tapestry of his life. He would have to mourn the loss of someone he wasn't allowed to name. Someone he could never talk about. In his mind, he held her close to him, letting her memory seep into his skin, settling there for what he hoped would be an eternity.

***

Derrien, now showered and changed after Ade had repaired his ankle in sick bay, had his hair cut off at once.

After seeing Geraint to his room, Owen came down the deck to visit Derrien, who was adjusting his new hairstyle and tie in the mirror.

"You're a new man," he said, watching him from the open doorway of the cabin. Derrien stared at himself in the mirror for a few seconds, studying the lines and cracks in his weatherbeaten face. The puffiness of his eyes had dissipated, though his heart was still shattered, scattering tiny fragments around as he breathed.

"I am. I mean to be," he said, looking at Thea's smiling face in the mirror. He turned to face her, but she had vanished again.

"I'm sure you will be," Owen said.

"Owen."

"Yeah?"

"What's going to happen to Anthony?"

Owen stopped and thought for a moment. "He's going to be fine. The surgeons back at Atlantis have a new heart already in the works. Since we left, no one has had any hallucinations— good news for him. As for the diplomatic mission we were supposed to be going on— the Athena has taken our place, thankfully. They were at each other's throats."

"I'm really sorry about that."

The two men stood in silence.

"The alien, Derrien. Is it really gone?" Owen asked, finally.

"Of course."

"Did you kill it?"

"Absolutely not."

Owen's gut lurched. "What did you do then?"

"We had an agreement. I let it go."

"What?" His blood ran cold. "Where?"

"Home."

***

Trin stepped out of the shower of her cabin and retrieved some underwear and clothes from her bedside drawers. She held the folded clothes to her face and inhaled the freshness. Her skin, although still wet, felt new. She patted her arms and legs down with the towel and dressed herself like it was the first time, savouring the cool caress of the clothes. Her new shirt felt soft and smooth, giving her skin space to breathe. She looked down at the crumpled heap of clothes she had sweated in for two days and shuddered. She picked them up and threw them into the laundry chute, slamming the hatch down with a bang.

A gentle knock at the door of her cabin caught her by surprise. She hurried to put some trousers on and hopped over to open it.

"Anthony!" she said, surprised to see him standing there. He had showered and dressed, and although he was undeniably striking in his uniform, he still looked tired and pale; she could see that there remained the residual handsomeness under the grey pallor. She smiled.

"Surprised to see me?" he asked, with one eyebrow raised.

"A bit, yes. I thought you were still in sick bay."

"Nah," he said, waving a hand. "Ade said I can go back to my room and rest."

She looked at him with an anticipation that was squeezing her chest. "And you came here because?"

"Because I want—I would like you to have dinner with me." He leaned into the doorway. She could smell his aftershave– an intoxicating citrusy musk with undertones of sandalwood.

"Now?"

"Only if you want to?"

"I do."

"Good," he said, stifling a grin. "I do also need to know... soy or pork?" He held up two ration packs and winked, much to her amusement.

***

Jet wearily laid his bag on the floor of his assigned cabin. Balthazar Swaine, realising Jet's situation, had guided him to the right room and showed him around. Jet was taken aback by the luxuriousness of the solid walls, air conditioning, new furniture and clean scent of the carpet. In the corner of his eye, a grey shape moved on the bed, startling him.

"Bojangles!" Balthazar screeched, pointing at the cat that lay on the bed. "I'm so sorry... Do you like cats?"

Jet shrugged. "I've never seen one before."

The grey tabby leapt from the bed and made a figure of eight around Jet's ankles, purring loudly. "He likes you," Balthazar said, scooping the feline up into his arms. The cat, on being manhandled, scrambled out of Balthazar's hold with a dramatic leap and a few scratches. "Ouch. Bojangles." Balthazar called after him. The cat scurried out of the room and back into the corridor, stopping to lick his paws. Jet smirked at the cat and then at Balthazar. Maybe he would like cats after all.

The small cabin on the Demeter was a million miles from his woodcutter's hut and even the cottage that the resident scientists had stayed in. "If there's anything else you need, you just call me on channel two." Balthazar said, reaching for the door. "I'm Cabin Steward Swaine."

Jet thanked him, sat down on the bed and waited for Balthazar to leave. When the door closed, he searched for something on his person. From his pocket he pulled out a tiny, sandy limpet shell and held it in his palm.

Coming January 2025: The Spider

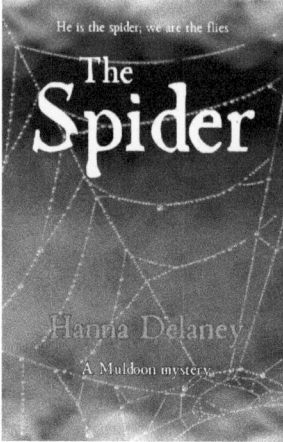

When Frances Bryant and her family arrive at their new home at number five, Percy Street, she doesn't feel welcome. Something lurks within the house, trying to catch her at every turn. What Frances discovers will force her to uncover the unforgivable, shattering the life she craves to pieces.

What begins as an encounter with the paranormal soon reveals itself to be a tangled web of secrets that Inspector Daniel Muldoon must get to the bottom of. Many lives hang in the balance, with two already claimed. Muldoon must compete in a race against time to save those who are still caught in the spider's web.

Pre-order the e-book now on amazon or get the paperback on 10th January 2025.

CHAPTER 1

L iverpool, 1892

Stepping out of the carriage to look at number five, Percy Street, Frances Bryant gasped. Her new home stood at an impressive four stories, with an ornate gabled roof and striking red brickwork. The beauty of it brought a lump to her throat. "This is our house?" she asked her husband, who was watching the nanny lift their daughter out of the carriage. The coach driver inspected the interior for any forgotten belongings and, satisfied that there was nothing there, gently closed the door, bowing to the little girl with a kind smile.

From the outside, the house was what her mother would have described as 'grand'. A grand house, with a green lawn, glistening white paint on the window frames and floors upon floors of space. It stood neatly contained among a row of complementary siblings, all proudly facing the street. Their gardens displayed their prosperity; their bricks displayed their wealth.

John Bryant stood beside his wife on the pavement, placing an arm around her waist. Frances felt that at any moment, she would wake up and be back in the cottage she had shared with her mother. "It's ours," John said, pointing the handle of his umbrella to the tall, black varnished door that stood within a pillared porch. "You can thank Australia." She looked up at his handsome, chiselled face. His grey eyes pierced through his tan like diamonds in the dirt. She felt a buzz of electricity power through her body as his lips landed on her cheek. She felt his moustache brush against her soft skin; although his new fashion statement tickled her, it added to his charming character, she thought. At that moment, they could have been the only people on the street, for she could see and love only him. Only one day before, it had been three years since she had last seen John Bryant.

"It feels like a dream."

Birds chirped in the dense trees overhead as the driver lifted their belongings out of the back of the cab. John ensured that the old man was paid and thanked. The horses, under firm instruction, trotted into action, taking the cab back the way they had come, leaving the Bryants and their nanny on the doorstep of number five. "Shall we?" John asked, raising an eyebrow.

"John, you're making me nervous," she said, taking to the steps with a giggle. He removed his hat and unlocked the door. Frances, on closer inspection, could see that it was freshly painted. "Don't touch it darling," she said to her little girl.

Elspeth 'Elsie' Bryant was four years old. She stood in a green velvet dress trimmed with black ribbon and held the hand of her nanny, Sarah Jones. Sarah, a young woman in her late twenties, had been an agreeable choice for a nanny when Elsie was a baby. More importantly, Elsie adored her. The family had been living in a small cottage in West Derby until John returned from Australia with what he called "a small fortune," and swiftly moved them to the eastern part of the city.

John stepped in first, hanging his hat on the stand. The black and white tiles that decorated the hall were brand new. "They finished just yesterday," John remarked as the women admired the craftsmanship. He hooked his umbrella on the coat stand and, as though he had lived there for years, checked himself in the hall mirror.

"John, this house is beautiful," Frances said, looking up at the white, high ceilings with their decorative cornices and festoons. The chandelier in the hall seemed enormous. She wanted to cry.

To Frances' surprise, waiting for them at the foot of the stairs were two women. The mid-morning sun had met the window of the landing, passing white beams down the stairs that silhouetted the two women at first. As her eyes adjusted to the light, Frances could see them in more detail. One was a young, thin maid with a pasty, freckled face and long, boney limbs. The other, an older lady. Both wore white lace caps and aprons. "Frances, this is our maid, Maggie," John said, introducing the first one.

"Good morning, Ma'am," Maggie said with a curtsey, revealing some rebellious strawberry blonde curls that tried to burst out on her return to standing upright. John raised an arm toward the older lady, "and this is Mrs Mckinnon, our housekeeper."

"Housekeeper?" Frances asked, taken aback by the announcement.

"Unless you want to run all of this by yourself, of course?" John opened his arms and twirled around the hallway. Frances shook her head. She did not want to manage four stories by herself.

"That's wonderful," she said. "Pleased to meet you. I'm Frances." she said, reaching out a hand. Mrs Mckinnon took it enthusiastically.

"It's lovely to meet you Mrs Bryant, Ma'am."

"Mrs Mckinnon and Maggie are with us every day except Sunday when they finish at twelve," John added. "The gardener comes every fortnight on a Monday."

"Wonderful," was all Frances could think to say. Mrs Mckinnon, almost sensing the impending silence, bent down to look at Elsie.

"And you must be Elspeth!" Mrs Mckinnon remarked, smiling at the little blonde girl hiding behind the nanny's skirts.

"Elsie can be quite shy, Mrs Mckinnon," said Sarah apologetically.

"Ach, I'm a strange old woman today. She'll get used to me, I'm sure." Mrs Mckinnon rummaged in her pocket and produced a small, boiled sweet. Elsie silently approached her and took the sweet like a little bird, retreating back to her hiding spot behind Sarah. Mrs Mckinnon laughed.

Frances took a moment to study the new housekeeper. Violet Mckinnon was a ruddy-faced Scotswoman in her fifties. She wore a tight silver bun at the nape of her neck and had a beautiful smile. She was a short, stout woman and had small, crescent glasses resting at the edge of her nose. "I wonder if anybody here likes scones? I make scones and cakes and buns, but only if everyone eats them."

"I'm sure that won't be a problem you're faced with," said Frances, looking back at Elsie who had reappeared from behind Sarah. Mrs Mckinnon laughed again. "Let us take the bags, Ma'am."

Without a word, Maggie stepped forward to collect a bag and took it upstairs, silently. She was gangly and thin but clearly she had hidden strength. Frances, aware of her own clumsy tendencies, stepped back, allowing them to gather the luggage without any obstacles and watched them disappear as they ascended the staircase.

"John," Frances whispered, "servants?"

He seemed surprised by her question. "Of course. I told you I wouldn't come back unless I could give you a better life. You and Elsie, that is."

"We can afford servants?"

"We can afford servants. They live downstairs in the basement, but there's a bell in every room should you need them outside of their duties."

Frances stared at him for a moment. He stood before her, pristinely dressed, moustache waxed , a new pocket watch and polished shoes. She looked down at her own clothes and cringed. She wore a grey wool travelling dress and old but well-loved boots. Her daughter, she noticed, was dressed better than she was. She felt out of place in the grand house as she caught herself in the mirror. Her face, although she felt it was amiable, looked tired.

Behind John stood a grandfather clock. Its hands were fixed on five minutes past twelve. "That's not the time, is it?" Frances asked. John retrieved his pocket watch from his jacket and checked.

"No, it needs winding," he said, removing his jacket and hanging it on the stand. He set to work on it immediately. "Well, don't wait for me. Go and explore," he said, noticing her still standing there watching him. Sarah, without a moment's pause, had followed Elsie out into the garden. Frances hung around for a moment longer before deciding on the parlour room.

As she had expected, it was a grand room with elegant furniture and a decorative fireplace that made her look twice. She found herself in the centre of the room, staring at it. The mirror above it bounced the light from the window into her eyes, blinding her. Rushing over to close the drapes, she clumsily crashed into a small ornament on the window ledge. "Oh no," she whispered as it fell onto the rug with a thud. It was a little figurine of a boy playing a flute. She inspected it quietly and sighed when she saw that he was still intact. Like a child wishing to hide their accidents from their mother, she looked over her shoulder and quietly, quickly restored him to his resting place. To her surprise, her hands were shaking.

She shuffled out of the room and back into the hallway. The ticking of the grandfather clock could be heard now. John closed the casing and took a cigar from the box on the sideboard of the hall, lighting it with a match from his pocket.

"Just needed winding," he said, admiring it. "Where have you been?"

"The parlour room, it's beautiful."

"I hoped you'd like it."

"I do!" she exclaimed. "It's almost as big as the entire cottage."

"You'll become accustomed, I'm sure," he said, inhaling some of the cigar and blowing it up into the air. "There's something you might like in the drawing room. Close your eyes."

With his cigar fixed firmly between his lips, he took her hands in his and gently guided her to the middle of the drawing room where she stood still, waiting.She could feel her heart thumping in her chest, not knowing what she was about to see.

"You can open them now."

The drawing room was large and well lit, with glass-panelled doors and a small garden outside. Frances spotted the cottage piano in the corner and clasped her hands over her mouth. John laughed at her reaction and lowered his cigar. "Well?" he asked.

"I haven't... I haven't played in years."

Since before they were married, she realised. It looked identical to the piano that her parents had when she was growing up; it was so old that she couldn't be sure that it *wasn't* the piano she had had growing up. Frances approached it excitedly and brushed a hand across the polished wood, smiling to herself as she did so. It seemed strangely familiar, compelling her to touch it.

"Are you going to play now?" John asked, leaning on the mantel-piece. She sat down on the stool with a thump, having misjudged the distance and after laughing at herself, lifted the lid carefully, tapping a couple of keys.

Eventually, a melody came to mind and she let her fingers explore the notes. She smiled to herself as she played.

CHAPTER 2

F rances hadn't noticed John's disappearance as she played her repertoire. *I don't blame him*, she thought. *I'm rather unpractised.* Wanting to see the rest of the house, she closed the lid over the keys and admired her piano one more time. She thought it was beautiful, but she wanted to see more of her new home and find where John had gone. With her skirts ruffling in the silence of the grand house, she ascended the stairs in search of him.

The master bedroom waited for her at the top of the first set of stairs. Inside it hung another chandelier above a four-poster bed. Her heart stopped when she came inside the room and saw the fresh rose petals on the linen. On the dresser was a decorative wooden box. She opened it gingerly. Inside were six chocolates. She took one and nibbled it.

She had not realised that John was waiting behind the door of the bedroom. "I hoped you'd find those," he said, closing it behind him. She gasped, and frightened by the sudden surprise, started choking on the chocolate she had just accidentally inhaled. She had not even sensed his presence, or smelled the cigar smoke. "I'm sorry," he said, laughing. "I didn't mean to scare you." The coughing finally ceased and they both laughed.

"Do you mean to kill me, John Bryant?"

"Absolutely not," he purred. "I didn't buy this house so I could be a widower in it." He took another pull from his cigar and released the clouds of smoke into the bedroom. Frances, having never been a fan of tobacco, went over to the other end of the room and opened the sash slightly. The hustle and bustle of the city outside quietly penetrated the silence of their bedroom. Sweet summer air blew in, replacing the slight staleness with a welcome freshness. She could see the river in the distance, twinkling in the peach haze of the afternoon sun as steamships sailed across the water. Out there, grey clouds of smoke from the factories rose into the sky as though from the nostrils of a sleeping dragon. In their house on the hill, she felt like a princess, gazing down at her kingdom from the comfort of her chambers. Miles of rooftops and greenery unfolded before her, rolling into the horizon like a watercolour painting.

"It's really something, John. I can't quite believe it." She looked out at the cobbled street and thought the rows of trees were so neat, like green beacons of hope standing up against the soot-covered buildings that she had been used to seeing on the waterfront. The comforting clip clop of hooves passing by reminded her that she was really there, really at home.

"It's all ours. There is one condition though."

Frances turned to look at him. His usual playful, carefree expression was partly obscured by heavy, downcast brows. She held her breath. He looked at her concerned face and smiled. "You must come to dinner with me whenever I ask."

Her shoulders relaxed and she shook her head. "Oh, desist with the games, John!" She walked over to the tall, oak wardrobe and inspected its contents. Various silks, furs and gowns hung from the rail, taking her aback. She didn't recognise any of them as hers. "John... are these–?"

"Yours? Of course they are. If we're going out to dinner, you'll need new dresses." He watched her pull out a red evening gown trimmed with lace and velvet. "I thought you'd like that one most of all." She held it to her chest and looked at herself in the tall mirror of the wardrobe. She thought that it was beautiful; she thought that *she* was beautiful.

"I do like it."

"Well, you can wear that one this week when I take you for dinner," he said, leaving the room. "Saturday night at the Adelphi hotel."

Frances smiled and placed the gown back into the wardrobe delicately. As she pushed the skirt back in, she noticed that it smelled different, with a whiff of a fragrance that she didn't recognise at first: Lavender. Realising that it had been so long since she had had new clothes, she wondered if the latest fashion was to have them made already perfumed. She looked down at her old, dull, woollen travelling gown and shrugged the notion off.

When she reached for the brass knob on the door of the bedroom, she was slowed by the sound of something creaking behind her. She sharply turned around to find that the door of the wardrobe was open, with the red skirt having unfolded and pushed its way out. She hurried back over to it and stuffed it in some more, closing the door firmly. She heard the magnet inside click and, satisfied with the second attempt at closure, left the room.

In the next room along the landing, there was a guest bed and some furniture similar to that of her bedroom. She walked in and went straight to the window. Elsie and Sarah were in the garden; Sarah had already drawn a hopscotch grid with chalk and was hopping across the squares much to Elsie's delight. Frances backed away from the window and sat down on the bed for a moment. The guest bedroom was another grand room, fragranced with various bowls and vases of dried flowers and herbs. Warm from the closed window and strong sunshine, Frances lay down on the bed and dozed.

She didn't know how long she had been sleeping for when she was awoken by the deafening whistle of the kettle.

Downstairs, Mrs Mckinnon had served tea in the parlour room. Frances thanked her graciously and rushed to sit down and pour herself a cup. John sat on the sofa opposite, reading a paper. She leaned back and admired him over the rim of her cup.

"See something you like?" he asked, not looking up. She laughed at having been caught.

"Yours is a face I have not seen for a long time, John Bryant. I was trying to etch it into my consciousness," she said quietly. He grinned and put the paper down on the coffee table.

"I'm not going anywhere, you know. At least not until winter."

"By then it shall be too soon."

"Are you happy here?"

"Incredibly so."

"Did you enjoy your sleep?"

"I didn't know I needed it."

"It pleases me to see how relaxed you feel here. I was worried you'd hate it."

"Why?"

"You were so used to the cottage. You were so used to your mother."

"She'll be all right. I've invited her here on Wednesday."

"Oh?"

"Don't look at me like that, John. She ought to see the house, don't you think?"

"I suppose. I wonder if I have an appointment on that day... all day perhaps," he said, rubbing his chin.

"John!"

"I'm teasing. I hope she likes it. Perhaps I'll go up in her estimations, who knows?"

Frances smiled and shook her head. "She must be impressed. It's not every day your daughter's husband returns from the other side of the world and surprises her with a house and servants."

"Good. It's all for you, you know." He sipped his tea and looked around the room. "I wanted it to be like new, as though I was bringing my new bride to her first house."

"We can pretend that that is exactly what this is."

"If you say so." He winked and reached for his paper again. "You like it then?"

"I think it's splendid," she said, fixing her gaze on the ornate mantelpiece once more. She was happier than she could find the words to express; not wanting to ruin the peace of the moment, she suppressed any further questions about Australia or his long absence and, knowing she had little will left to avoid talking about it, filled her twitching mouth with tea instead of words.

The clock in the hallway began to chime, which surprised Frances as she glanced at the mantle clock that said it was half past two in the afternoon. The chimes continued. She listened, counting them.

"That blasted clock," John said, slamming the paper down on the table. "It's stuck on twelve again."

"Perhaps we need it mended," she said.

"Perhaps we need it hammered to pieces," he said, rolling his sleeves up. With a look of disdain, he marched out of the room.

— · —

Chapter 3

F rances, having not yet explored the nursery, ventured upstairs. When she reached the top of the second staircase, she found that there was a long landing with only one door at the end. The long wall was adorned with various paintings of people and places. Much smaller copies of famous works by Monet and more recent impressionists whose names she couldn't remember stood proudly, overlooking the highest floor of the house in gilded frames.

"Elsie?" she asked, "are you there?" She slowly approached the panelled door and listened first. Frances reached for the knob and turned it clockwise. The door opened with ease as she peered in to see an empty nursery.

Frances looked across the room to the open window, still unable to accept that this was her view now. Across the street, there were passers by walking on the pavement and conversing outside the church. Horses trotted past carrying various loads, nodding as they pulled their carriages, trams and carts to their destinations. Everything was as expected, but a part of her felt that it would all fall away and reveal itself to have been merely a trick: something that could have been, not something that *was*.

Burying the doubt once more, she turned around to look at the nursery again. It looked as though Sarah and Elsie had already explored their new rooms, placing their things on the beds and changing out of their travel clothes. Frances picked up Elsie's little green dress from the bed and hung it in the wardrobe that stood against the partition wall to Sarah's bed. Frances, on closer inspection, thought that the side room where Sarah slept was cleverly designed; Elsie could have her own room with her nanny always within arm's reach.

Unlike other parts of the house, it was not the fumes of fresh paint that reached her nostrils in this room, it was a floral fragrance. As with her bedroom on the first floor, there were bundles of potpourri stationed on every surface, resting in little dishes on dressers and above the wardrobe. They smelled of rosemary and lavender. She thought of the red dress and suspected that there was potpourri in her wardrobe, too.

The teddy bears and rocking horse reminded her of her own nursery when she was small. She pushed the horse gently and watched it glide back and forth on its runners. Its expression, although carved and permanently set, seemed cheerful.

She loved the nursery. It had plenty of room for play. As she admired the tedd

bears of various shapes, colours and sizes, Frances wondered if they would have any more children to fill the enormous room with. Elsie had been their only child due to John's work arrangements. The thought of being alone for several years more made her shudder. She wondered if that was over now as she examined the toys and the furniture in the room. There were so many toys. Too many for one girl.

The little bed where her daughter would sleep had a curtained canopy. Elsie had called it a "princess bed." Frances sat down on it and admired the decor and linens of the room. John really had thought of everything. Rows of pretty dolls sat against a wall, each decorated with their own frilly frocks, bows and bells. Frances admired them all, wondering how much John had had to pay for them. He hadn't discussed specific numbers but, judging from the clothing she had seen and the house he had just moved them to, she felt that it must have been enough to buy all of these toys as well. She picked one of the little dolls up and held it. It had tight black curls and blue glass eyes that stared back at her.

"That's Blissy," said a little voice behind her. Frances felt her heart leap and kick back into action again as she looked down at her daughter.

"Goodness, you scared Mummy, sweetheart."

"Blissy is new. She has lots of sisters," Elsie said calmly. She was wearing a lighter, blue frock with a broderie anglaise skirt. It was incredibly similar to the frilly dress that Blissy was wearing. Frances looked back at her daughter and then at the dolls sitting against the wall.

"Oh she certainly does, doesn't she? How are they all feeling about the new house?"

"It's not new for them," Elsie said. Frances felt her blood run cold. "They've been here for a long time."

Their strange conversation was abruptly executed when the little bell on the wall of the nursery rang. Frances, not knowing what it meant, slowly approached the landing, held her breath and listened. Downstairs, she could hear the kettle whistling again.

Frances sat at the kitchen table with Elsie while Sarah prepared supper for her, making some tea for Frances in the process. Frances thanked her and took the cup gratefully, sipping on the steaming liquid. Despite the summer evening sunshine outside, she felt chilled to the bone.

"Ach, you should have let me do that, Sarah," said Mrs Mckinnon, entering the room with a basket of fruit and vegetables in her arms. She laid it down on the kitchen table. Elsie's eyes lit up at the sight of cherries, which rested with their shiny red skins atop cabbages and turnips. Mrs Mckinnon wiped her hands on her apron and poured a cup for Sarah. "Tomorrow, I'll bake some scones," she said. "How would you like that, Elsie?"

Elsie nodded.

"Good."

"Thank you, Mrs Mckinnon," Frances said, looking at the basket of food, "that would be nice."

"I can't wait to sleep in the princess bed," Elsie said, eating her toast.

Frances thought of Elsie's pretty little bed. "When I was a little girl, I'd have loved nothing more than a princess bed," she replied. "You are a very lucky girl, Elsie. Daddy bought this house and decided that you would have a princess bed. How lucky you are."

"Maybe Daddy is a king."

"Maybe he is."

"And Mummy is a queen."

Frances brought the cup to her lips and, in a moment of absent-mindedness, scalded her top lip on the tea. She flinched and licked her lip, lowering the cup back down to the table. As she blew tendrils of steam away from it, she noticed something laced around the inside of the china cup: it looked like a crack. She blew some more until it was safe to investigate with a finger. On closer inspection, she saw a long thread of dark brown hair with amber flecks that caught the fading light of the sun. Sarah, who had been watching in horror, apologised. "I didn't see, ma'am."

Frances looked around at her daughter and Sarah. Sarah's mousy, light brown hair was tied up in a braid; mother and daughter were blonde; Mrs Mckinnon's hair was unquestionably grey.

Later that evening, Frances came to say goodnight to Elsie in the nursery. When she reached the top step of the landing, she smiled at the sound of Elsie's little voice, deep in conversation with someone. Frances crept around the corner to see if she could catch a glimpse of the imaginary discussion, as she always enjoyed doing. Elsie was talking to a teddy bear on her bed. Sarah was on the other side of the room folding clothes into a drawer.

"It's time to go to sleep, Finn," she heard her daughter say to the bear. "There's nothing to be afraid of."

Frances' stomach sank with sadness at the thought of anyone being afraid of the dark. She wondered if the bear was acting as a vessel for her daughter's worries and decided to step in. "Nobody's afraid of the dark in here, are they?"

Elsie shook her head. "Finn was, but he's not any more."

"I'm glad to hear it, Finn." Frances looked down at the tatty golden bear in her daughter's arms.

"Mummy," Elsie began, "are you afraid of the dark?"

"No, darling. I'm not afraid of the dark."

"Mary is."

"Is she?"

"Yes. The dark is when she's alone."

Frances' and Sarah's eyes met, locking for a moment. Sarah feigned a smile and said, "I'm sure Mary will be fine, Elsie. Don't worry about such things." She closed the drawer and came to the bedside. "Give your Mummy a kiss and say goodnight. We have church tomorrow, don't forget. A piano lesson, too."

Frances leaned in and kissed Elsie's forehead. "Goodnight sweetheart."

"Goodnight, Mummy."

Frances nodded to Sarah and left the room, closing the nursery door behind her. The sconces on the landing flickered slightly with the backdraft of the closed door, casting long, erratic shadows across the walls.

The dark is when she's alone.

Frances shook her head. "Childish nonsense," she whispered to herself.

She descended the staircase and shot a look across her shoulder despite herself. The landing was still, with a sliver of golden light stretching from underneath the nursery door. She went downstairs in silence.

If you loved this, pre-order your copy now!

ABOUT THE AUTHOR

Hanna lives in her home city of Liverpool with her husband and three kids. She loves dogs, books, running, gaming and can't resist a ghost story. She studied English Literature BA and went on to complete a Literature MA at Liverpool Hope University before teaching English for several years. Oceanus- a re-imagining of The Tempest is her debut novel. You can catch up with Hanna and see what she's working on at hannadelaneyauthor.com

Sign up to the newsletter for exclusive fiction in your inbox!

ACKNOWLEDGEMENTS

Writing a novel is no mean feat, and it can be a solitary existence when you're writing one. Firstly, my husband, who supported every idea, every draft and every moment that I needed to spend writing— thank you. I appreciated every proofreading session, every comment, and every critique. I would also like to thank my Substack subscribers and the wider fiction community of Substack. You are some of the most wonderful, encouraging people to be around. Thank you to Michele Bardsley for taking a new novelist under your wing and for helping me see the road ahead. Thank you to Michael and Lesley Gough, Alexandra Gilligan-Cook, Christina Murray, Autumn Thomson and Sue Burch. I hadn't shown you any of my novel yet but you immediately stepped forward and said "I'm backing this project." Thank you for taking a chance on me. Thank you to my best friend, Suzanne, who once said, "there are worse books out there, do you know what I mean?"— you're an absolute hero and I think about this every time I write. Thank you to Lee Robinson who made sure that I had an author website in order to look 'the real deal'. I am very much aware that this was not a horror novel but I couldn't write this page without also mentioning the Macabre Monday team on Substack who welcomed me into the writing community with open arms. I will be forever grateful for your kindness and enthusiasm. I'll end with an additional special mention for Ika, Evelyn, Liz, Rob, David, Jim, Ken and last but not least, Vulkan, who asked to be babe dropped. There are many, many people I would like to thank for helping me see this through but it's not possible to name them all individually. This will have to do.

Milton Keynes UK
Ingram Content Group UK Ltd.
UKHW041813151124
451262UK00005B/516

9 798227 550156